The Runaway Settlers

The Runaway Settlers

AN HISTORICAL NOVEL

by *Elsie Locke*

Illustrated by Antony Maitland

E. P. DUTTON & CO., INC.

NEW YORK

67-7682

+

Contents

New Zealand

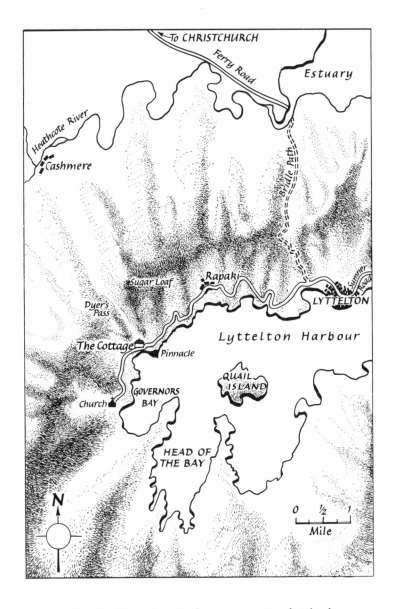

Detail of Lyttelton Harbour area on South Island

Because this is a book about a real family, we shall begin with introductions. The story starts in New South Wales, Australia, in March 1859 – more than a hundred years ago.

The parents are Mary Elizabeth Small and Stephen Small. There is a grown-up daughter, Mary Ann, and the ages of the children are: Bill, fifteen; Jack, twelve; Archie, nine; Jim, seven; Emma, two.

E. L.

I

The Australian Farm

ARCHIE SMALL squatted beside the hutch where he kept his pet ring-tailed possum and told his little sister Emma, for the fourth time, a long story about how he had put the rings on the tail himself. The possum could not be bothered any more to eat the strips of carrot which they passed through the wire. It had been a long and dismal day, with Archie having to mind Emma, and Jim so sick they weren't even allowed in his room, and Emma crying for her mother who had gone away in such a hurry. The only way Archie could think of to comfort her was to show her the animals he loved – the parrots in the trees, the late calves in the paddock and the lizards asleep on the dry logs.

Now the delicious smell of hot beef stew came drifting through the rickety doors of the farmhouse. Archie lifted his nose to enjoy that smell and bounded inside. But his big sister Mary Ann was not dishing up. She was pushing the swinging iron pans to the side of the fireplace.

"Aren't we to have it yet?" he asked shyly, for he was a little afraid of Mary Ann, who was like a second mother in the house but had not yet learned to be kind when she was stern.

Mary Ann brushed the hair back from her sweating face. She hardly seemed to notice that he was there. "I must see if Mother is coming," she said, and went outside, leaving Archie to enjoy nothing more than another whiff of that beautiful smell. He went back slowly to Emma and the possum.

From the veranda Mary Ann looked out over her mother's gay garden, past the orange trees and the peach trees and the rolling pastures with their patches of blue-gum. The track could be seen at several points, but there was no sign of anyone. Only her brother Bill, dark and strong and already taller than she, came from the calf paddock with the empty buckets.

"Isn't she home?" he called.

Mary Ann's voice trembled. "Oh Bill – I'm that feared! What if she never comes back? Why did she have to go?" Then to Bill's consternation – for she hardly ever cried – she sat down on the steps and sobbed into her apron. He sat beside her, not knowing what to say, or *how* to tell of the wild plans that had haunted his mind all through this long and wretched day.

His father had risen early and mustered the young cattle for selling far inland, where the prices were good. He had driven off in the buggy with his riding horse tied behind, and the two blackfellows alongside to help with the mob. The children had rejoiced silently to see him go – until at the last minute Mother had come out wearing her town dress and telling some story about needing to buy braid and buttons. This did not sound like a real reason: not after last night! If Father's drunken rage had gone only a little further, then Jack and Jimmy might have been killed, instead of being knocked up so badly that they were kept in their beds all day. How many bruises Mother had, under those long sleeves and long skirts, no one could guess. Yet she had left them all, with two boys flat on their beds, to go with Father! And what if he had turned upon her somewhere on that lonely way into Berrima?

"Don't cry, Mary Ann," said Bill. "She'll come, and Father will be miles away, and we won't see him for a week."

"A week!" cried Mary Ann. "He'd do better to lose himself in the desert and never come back. And the cattle with him. He loves *them* at least! Every care for the stock while the house is crumbling to pieces and we haven't a stitch to go out in looking decent!"

"He looks after the cattle 'cause there's money in them," said Bill.

Mary Ann looked at him sideways. Was he sticking up for Father? But he'd been down in the paddocks last night, and hadn't seen what went on; the worst scene they'd ever had. Stephen Small had seized a chair and struck his wife to the floor, and Jack, trying to get in between, had taken the next blows until his shoulder and arm were paralysed with the bruises. Mary Ann, following her mother's orders, had lifted Emma and run to the bush to hide, with Archie at her heels; but Jim, pinned to the floor by fear, had been picked up and hurled against the wall where he had lain white and still, with not enough breath left for crying. Through the whole day he could scarcely be roused to take a drink of water.

11

"Bill, you go look at Jim," she said sharply. "It might be you next."

"Oh no it won't!" The words came out in a rush. "See here! I'm going away."

"Away? You?"

"Yes, me. To the goldfields!"

He couldn't mean it! Bill, the only one who was anything like a man to protect them all! Mary Ann turned on him with scorn.

"Stuff and nonsense! The goldfields? They don't give any licences to boys of your age!"

"There's jobs a-plenty to be had, helping out. And any rate you can say what you like, I'm going to run away."

"Then you must take us all along with you, Bill," said a gentle voice behind them, "for we're all of us going to run away."

"Mother!" Mary Ann jumped up with gladness.

Mrs Small was standing in the doorway. She had returned unseen, and already looked at the sleeping Jimmy, and made Jack's arm comfortable upon a pillow. Her clothes were dusty from her long walk, but she was smiling.

"I'm sorry, Mother," said Bill, half-ashamed, half-defiant, "but I can't stand any more of it!"

"Nor can the rest of us, Bill. I'm not teasing! We will *all* run away – but not, I think, to the goldfields. I've bidden your father a longer goodbye than he knows; and I've seen the coaching agent in Berrima, for we're to travel tomorrow morning."

"And Father consented!" Mary Ann was astonished.

"Oh no!" Mrs Small's face creased all over with smiles, and suddenly Mary Ann thought how pretty she looked, with her blue eyes and chestnut hair, and her worries thrown recklessly away. "He thinks I've come home with my buttons and braid, and, dear me, I quite forgot to buy them. The droving will keep him for a week. A week's grace we have, to be away to a place where he'll never find us. Never again!"

"But what if he does find us? And Mother, how will we manage? Where will we go?"

"Can anything be worse, my dear, than staying here?"

She put her hand on the girl's arm as if to say, "Have courage!" But before she could say more, they heard the joyful squeals of Archie and Emma, who had seen their mother and come running; happy because she was home, and because the stew over the kitchen fire would be something more than a most delicious smell.

Jack Small rolled over on his stretcher-bed and at once began to dream. He was falling over a steep bank into the Wingecarribee River – rolling and bumping his shoulder; and when he looked up and tried to call for help, there was his father leaning over the bank and grinning horribly. He hit the bottom but it wasn't the river, it was a floor, with a goanna crawling out of a crack towards him. When he tried to shout, "Go away!" the words came out as dry grunts, and he saw that it was no goanna but his brother Jim lying curled and limp against the wall. Jack reached out his hand and there was his father in between, still grinning horribly. He tried once more to bawl, "Go away!" and woke up.

It was not his father standing there, but his mother in her white apron, holding a candle in one hand and a plate in the other.

"Don't be troubled, Jack," she said kindly. "You've lain

over on your sore shoulder and got to dreaming. But we can't let you lie abed, for we shan't have time to spare, with the coach due to leave at nine. You must grin and bear that sore shoulder. Now have your breakfast, so we can be washed up and away."

Jack struggled up and began on the heated-up stew, fried potatoes and milk. Through the doorway he could see Mary Ann wrapping plates in tea-towels and putting them in the big wooden chest with the name LONDON still showing from the old voyage. She had been busy with brooms and buckets all night; for if Father came back to an empty house, it still had to be a clean one. Jack reached under the mattress with his good arm and drew out his belt and his sheath-knife.

Mrs Small had to dress Jim as if he were a baby, he was so dazed; and she had to help Jack too, and put his sore arm in a sling. In the dawn light, Bill made ready the hand-cart, which was all they had, since Father had taken the buggy. They piled it high with boxes, carpet-bags, two rolls of blankets, and one billy with bread and cold meat for the journey, and another packed with fresh eggs. ("A present for someone," Mrs Small said mysteriously.) Last of all, Bill turned the calves in with the cows and opened the fowl-yard gate. Wouldn't Father be furious if they all went bush! But they must find their own food and water now.

Everyone had taken a special treasure. Mary Ann carefully wrapped a silk handkerchief around the brooch and locket sent by her aunt in England, Bill had his set of draughts, Jack his knife, Jim his stuffed koala and Emma her rag doll, Bibi. Only Archie was in trouble, for his treasure was alive. He stood in front of the hutch and stroked the barred tail of the possum.

"Archie, you must open the door and let him go," called his mother. "They wouldn't allow him in the coach."

"We could hide him in a billy," pleaded Archie.

"They'd hear him scratching, stupid," said Jack.

"I could put him with the clothes in the carpet-bag!"

"He'd make a fine mess of the clothes – ugh! I'll catch you another one, Archie, when we get there."

Archie was not to be trapped.

"Will there be ring-tails where we're going? Will there?"

Mrs Small puckered her face while she thought of an answer.

"I'm not sure. But there'll be something for a pet, be sure of that! Your possum will be happy in the trees, now he's grown big. He wouldn't be happy shut up in a bag, would he?"

But Archie was still clinging to the hutch when the hand-cart was pushed through the gate; then he flung open the cage door, sobbing, and raced after the others as his pet came slowly out and sat on top of the cage, not able to believe in his freedom.

The house, with its bare slab walls and bark roof, looked more dreary than ever. Mrs Small had a last friendly look at the geraniums, the tall lilies, and the blaze of bottlebrush on the hedge. Her flowers could run wild now, or be smothered by the weeds, and she could not stop them.

"I shall make a garden that beats this one," she said cheerily.

All the same, she closed the gate so that the cattle should not get in to chew the flowers; and took Archie by the hand, to comfort him for his greater loss.

2

Escape to Sydney

To reach Berrima, there was first their own track and then the side road, which was scarcely any smoother. The hand-cart had to be dragged over ruts and roots, uphill and downhill, through patches of bush and above the river, with Emma and Jim both riding on top. Jack could help a little with his good arm; but nearly all the effort must come from Bill, Mary Ann and Archie. Mrs Small did not speak of her own bruises, but the children guessed at the reason why she, usually so strong, did not offer to lend a hand.

Emma broke into the high-pitched, droning song that showed she was happy. This was too much for Mary Ann, who felt anything but joyful. She had been up all night, cleaning and packing; and she was haunted by a fear that at any moment their father might appear and confront them. Every knot of trees and every shoulder of a hill was a dangerous spot. To keep from stumbling on the rough road in her high-buttoned boots and long skirts, she kept her gaze downwards. Across her vision the trousered legs of her brothers moved steadily to and fro.

"Mother," she cried in envy, "why weren't *we* born boys!"

"We, Mary Ann? And if I'd been born a boy, you wouldn't have been born at all!"

"Then we should all wear trousers, like the Japanese."

"Chinese," said Mrs Small.

"How could you wear trousers?" scoffed Jack. "You'd be worse than the blacks!"

Archie and Bill laughed at this, for the aborigine women wore scarcely anything at all. As for their babies, they were quite naked as they peeped over their mothers' shoulders to watch the Small family go by. Two of their men had gone to help Stephen Small with the cattle, and now here was a curious thing – the white woman and all her children going walk-about! But they asked no questions, and nobody stopped to explain.

Tears welled up in Mary Ann's eyes. She was weary and frightened, but more than that, she was ignorant. She hadn't known the difference between Japanese and Chinese! She had learned to read and write at the kitchen table when the day's work was done, but there were never any new books to read. Perhaps where they were going there would be a library at least? Oh, they must hurry, and be sure to reach Berrima in time for the coach!

At this thought she began to stride out so strongly that

Archie protested – he couldn't keep up! So Mrs Small began to sing in her clear, strong voice:

"In Dublin's fair city, where the girls are so pretty,
   I first set my eyes on sweet Molly Malone,"

and they all joined in:

"She wheeled her wheelbarrow, through streets broad and
   narrow,
   Crying cockles, and mussels, alive, alive-O."

It was as good as a band, for marching along.

Although Berrima was one of the oldest inland settlements in Australia, the homesteads were scattered and there were few people to ask where the Smalls were going. When they did, Mrs Small had a simple answer. They were taking Jim to Sydney to see the doctor. Poor little fellow, he'd had a fall, and who could tell what that might lead to? If anybody wondered why the doctor in Berrima was not good enough, or why they needed to take the boxes and bags, or why Bill and Mary Ann weren't left to care for the house and the animals, nobody really asked such questions. Stephen Small was well known for his drunken rages, and it might be best not to know too much if his wife and children took a journey during his absence.

At Berrima the hand-cart was unloaded and left standing empty. Outside the Surveyor's Rest Hotel, the coach was waiting – a splendid sight that sent Emma off on another bout of her droning song. The four horses, three brown and one grey, allowed Archie to stroke their noses and leaned over for more. The seven Smalls almost filled the seats of the coach. The other places were taken by a gentleman in a top hat and

gloves, and a lady in a blue silk dress and paisley shawl, too
fine to speak to this farm woman with the workworn hands
or her daughter in a bonnet completely out of fashion.

For their part, the Smalls were too excited to notice anything but the changing countryside; and jubilant too, for they
were fast moving in the opposite direction from their father.
In truth, every jolt of the iron wheels against the stones of the
road sent spasms of pain through the sore bodies of Jack and his
mother, although Jim, with his eyes closed, did not seem to
wake sufficiently to feel anything. But physical pain was not
enough to dampen the excitement of the journey. Mary Ann
called out with joy whenever she recognized a scene she remembered from the out-coming journey, ten years before,
after sailing from England. There were forests and townships
and still more forests, until they came through Parramatta and
its deep cutting and on to a hill with the great city spread out
before them, and the shining blue harbour.

Even Mary Ann was silent at the size of it all. Many ships
lay at the wharves, or rode at anchor, or sailed towards the
open sea. Tier upon tier the buildings rose up the hills, from
tiny cottages to two-storeyed mansions with tower windows;
inns and auction-rooms and banks and merchants' offices, built
of stone or brick; churches with tall spires; shops with windows filled with goods, not jumbled all together as in the
Berrima store, but each displaying its own specialty of elegant
clothes, or saddles and harness, or tools, or jewellery, or toys.
When the coach stopped at last a window directly opposite
was set out with little dishes of gold, coarse and fine and scaly,
and nuggets as big as Emma's fingers. A notice declared that
gold would be bought at the best prices. Diggers went in and
out, looking very fine in their town suits of serge, their leather

belts and slouched hats, and the gold watch-chains across their waistcoats.

Bill couldn't stop staring.

"Mother, the goldfields! Look, that's where they get their fortunes – that's where the money is!"

Busy gathering her boxes and bags together, Mrs Small paused as a tall bearded man strode by.

"He'll be pawning that watch-chain and the watch too, I shouldn't wonder, before the year's out. Easy come, easy go, that's the way of the diggings, Bill."

"They say if you strike it lucky, you make a hundred pounds in a day!"

"And what if you strike it unlucky and lose the shirt off your back?"

"I'd start digging somewhere else!"

"No, Bill. A goldfield's a place where you plunder the ground, and move on. What we want is a home, a real home. A place to put my foot down."

"I'll bet you don't know where to find it," teased Jack.

"Somewhere there's a corner made specially for us."

"I wish it could be here!" said Mary Ann.

A cabriolet with a smart driver wearing kid gloves had just drawn up, and into this stepped the lady and gentleman who had travelled in the coach. It set off down the street at a pace that made the coach look old and clumsy – which, in fact, it was. A still grander carriage swept by in the other direction. There was a glimpse of a fashionable lady and her daughters; and riding on the back was a footman, in braided jacket and silk stockings! And Mary Ann stood there in her plain grey dress and her out-of-date bonnet.

If only we could live in Sydney! she thought. But Father would surely find us in the end.

Mrs Small made arrangements for the boxes to be kept until called for, and helped Jim to ride pick-a-back with Bill. She shook her head when Bill asked if they could take a cab instead; and Jack, sore as he was, agreed with her that it was safest to walk.

"Father might trace us by the cab. We'd be caught like rats in a hole!"

"Is there somewhere for us to go?" whispered Archie, troubled.

"Yes, Archie," said Mrs Small. "I'll tell you now: we have a secret friend."

"Secret! Does she know about *you*?"

"Yes – she was my friend at school, in London. That's who the eggs are for. But Father doesn't know I was sending money, little by little, to be saved until there should be enough for us to come."

"It's all been planned!" cried Bill, disappointed because he thought it was his idea first, this running away.

"But we won't be staying?" asked Jack.

"First we'll go to our secret friend. Then I really will take Jim to a doctor, for I think he's very sick. Then" – she pointed to the harbour – "on a ship."

"To Victoria!" Bill said eagerly.

"No, Bill, not *those* goldfields either."

Bill went quiet. His mother would never go to the goldfields, but the time would come when she couldn't stop him from going, he told himself.

Emma began to sing:

"A ship, a ship, a ship!"

"Will we go back to England?" asked Mary Ann.

"There's not enough money for so long a journey. No! We must go where we can. We may count on five days more till your father knows – only five days. Tomorrow, if the doctor says it's safe for Jim to travel – and I pray that he will – I shall visit the shipping offices. Bill – how are you managing with Jim? Shall we take a rest?"

"People keep looking at us," said Archie.

"Then we shall rest a little, on the bench outside that inn over there!"

They sat down, and Jack broke the silence.

"So we don't know where we're going!"

"Today, yes. Next week, let's say –"

"We're going to seek our fortunes."

"That's right, Jack."

"Fortoons, fortoons," sang Emma, not knowing in the least what it was all about.

They went on, round corners and along winding streets, till they came to the secret friend. Her name was Mrs Mc-Cracken and she lived in a long white house with lace curtains, and crocheted counterpanes, and a piano, and gaslight, and windows overlooking the harbour. On the veranda, to the delight of Archie, there swung a cage with a canary singing at the top of his voice.

Mrs McCracken came to the door wearing a lace cap. Dimples rippled over her cheeks and chin.

"Mary Elizabeth Small!" she cried. "Oh, you've come at last! Safe and sound! Oh, it's too much to believe!"

She swung little Emma up in a cosy hug, and welcomed every one of them into the house. Then she bustled off to bake an enormous apple pie.

3

Ships and Donkeys

THE doctor was cheerful about Jim. Concussion, that was what ailed him: a little more rest would put him right. Within another day, Jim's old impish ways were returning, and it was hard for Mrs McCracken to keep him in bed, even with marvels like picture-books and a stereoscope to look through. When a picture was put into the stereoscope, it made the people look so tall and so near, they seemed to be walking out towards him.

Sydney was exciting and bewildering, with so much to see in the streets. Mrs Small took the boys out to buy new trousers and jackets. "We can't go to another home looking poverty-stricken," she said. Cotton print was bought too, and Mary

Ann made dresses for Emma and herself, with help from Mrs McCracken on her sewing-machine. Emma watched by the hour and wanted to poke her fingers in the wheel, for she had never seen a sewing-machine before.

But there was no success in the search that really mattered – the search for a ship. True, the harbour was full of ships; but every one of them was tied up for a long time, or privately chartered, or carrying cargo only, or bound for some impossible place like China or Peru. Mrs Small went the rounds of the shipping offices, and Mr McCracken, who worked in a bank, used all his influence; then Bill and Jack were sent to the wharves to ask of the seamen; but there was no passage to be had. And soon there were only three days left before Stephen Small would come home and find them gone! He would saddle his horse and ride, and even the great city with its hundreds of houses might not be enough to hide his family.

On the fourth day Archie, who hated being kept in the big house even with a canary on the veranda, asked if *he* might go and find a ship. The others thought this a great joke, as if ships could be found hiding under leaves, like snails or spiders! Archie shrank inside, went silent and ran off without permission. When he did not come back, Bill and Jack were sent to look for him.

Round broad streets and narrow lanes they went asking if anyone had seen a nine-year-old boy with sandy hair and blue eyes; but the people only said no – but surely he was old enough to ask his way home? And for fear that their own father might soon be asking these very questions, they did not like to say that they came from the outback. They had almost decided to go back when Jack stopped short.

"Listen, Bill! It's a donkey!"

"In Sydney? Don't be daft!"

"But it is – look there."

They looked down on an empty section filled with tall grass and weeds, and saw not one donkey, but four of them. The braying came from one grey fellow who was being beaten by two men in a vain effort to make him move. There was a big, dark man in a blue-and-white-striped jersey, and another in a sea-jacket. The more they yelled and swore, the more stubborn grew the donkey.

"Huh!" said Bill. "Archie could do better than that."

It was a prophecy. From behind a stump overgrown with creepers appeared a familiar figure. He stood beside the smallest donkey, a white one, stroking it and talking softly. Soon he had it walking quietly. Bill and Jack, moving closer, heard Archie say:

"Where d'you want them to go, mister?"

The man in the striped jersey swung around.

"Who in tarnation are you?"

Archie grinned shyly, not knowing what to say. "You meddling limb of Satan!" shouted the man. "Aren't donkeys devils enough!" Archie's grin vanished but he went on stroking the donkey. The man in the sea-jacket stepped in.

"Whisht, Rabbie! Dinna curse at the lad; we could mebbe let him show what he can dae! Try if ye can move her doon the street there, laddie."

"Bill," whispered Jack, "this looks like fun! Let's go too."

Bill nodded. "There might be a shilling for us. But take off that sling – it doesn't look right."

Jack winced as the arm swung free and dragged at his bruised shoulder, but he said nothing except a quick, "We'll help, mister, we're his brothers," without waiting for an answer.

Soon a little procession was moving down the hill. Even the stubborn grey donkey, with the two men urging him, followed on.

"Where d'you want them to go?" called Archie.

"To the wharves," answered the man in the striped jersey.

The wharves! With wild excitement leaping inside him, Jack cut in: "Are they to go on a ship?" and Bill and Archie held their breath for the answer.

"Yes, a ship. Pedigree stock they are – special purchase – for the *Armenian*."

"The *Armenian*!" The boys had not tramped the wharves for nothing. "We've seen her – she's a capital ship – with engines!"

"Aye," said the man in the sea-jacket, "but we maun get the beasties aboard, afore those engines'll be any use at all!"

A bold thought began to grow in Jack's mind.

Stockmen! They might need stockmen on the ship!

The *Armenian* lay alongside the wharf, not at anchor in the harbour as the bigger sailing-ships usually did, because she had this very modern feature: an engine, sixty horse-power, no less! She was square-rigged too, and the wind would carry her much faster than her screws, but the engine made her more easily handled in harbour and for this reason she was given the proud title of steamship. She was well-appointed too, with fine cabins for the gentlemen and ladies, who were all on shore somewhere until near the time for sailing.

Obediently, with Archie and his white donkey still in the lead, the animals went up the gangway and into their pen on the deck. There were large stalls, too, in readiness for larger animals – horses.

And now Robbie and his Scotch companion, whose name was Dugald, found that it was not enough to offer the boys a shilling for their trouble. They all said no – that this was not what they wanted.

"What would ye be wanting then?" asked Dugald.

"To look after the donkeys on the voyage," said Bill calmly.

The two men looked at one another as if they didn't know whether to laugh or not, and the big man winked.

"Oh! Ye'll be running away then, will ye?"

"That's right."

"And the wee laddie too?"

"I'm not wee, I'm nine," said Archie. Dugald ignored him.

"And yer mither and yer sister, I don't doot," said the sailor sarcastically.

"Two sisters – " Jack could not help grinning. "And *Jim*!" shouted all three boys together.

The gentle rolling of the ship seemed to break into a mad rocking with their burst of laughter. When at last they recovered, Dugald said:

"Would that be the lot noo? Ye havena' a father, maybe?"

"No, mister. We haven't any father," said Bill.

"Our mother's a widow. We have to look after her," Jack added quickly, thinking this might help. Dugald was at once sympathetic.

"Ah, puir laddies! But will ye no be scared to travel on a ship with Indians?"

"Indians!" They had no idea what an Indian would be like. "Are they black men?"

"Aye, black – or brown maybe."

"We're not scared of blacks. We had them working on the farm – when – when – we had our father."

"But is the ship going to India?" Mrs Small might refuse to

go to Victoria but she would like India no better, Bill felt sure. To his relief the men laughed loudly at this one, too.

"No! Not India. That's where we've come from."

"Is Armenia a country?" asked Archie shyly.

"Aye, Armenia's a country, but she won't be going there neither," said Robbie. "She's bound for Lyttelton, New Zealand."

"New Zealand! How d'ye like the sound o' that, laddies?"

Dugald looked keenly to see what impression he had made. He expected that all this nonsense would end with the mention of a country so small and far away, but only Bill showed a flicker of disappointment. Jack said at once:

"We like it! Where is Lyttelton anyway?"

Seeing the men choke back their laughter, he didn't wait for an answer but hurried on: "We're very experienced with stock, sir. Donkeys, cattle, horses!"

"There'll be horses, fifty-five of 'em, tomorrow; and then we sail. Well! You'd best ask the boss. He'll be down soon, I daresay, to see the donkeys are in good shape. They're wanted for the breeding of mules, for the whole country's tipped on end with rocks all over the place, and nothing else can get over them. And you'll best mind your p's and q's, for he's a famous gentleman – a judge that had thousands of lives in the palm of his hand, in the Indian troubles. You'll touch your cap when you meet Mr John Cracroft Wilson."

"I haven't got a cap," said Jack.

"More's the pity, for this is him coming now, if I'm not much mistaken."

The judge, looking perfectly at ease on a splendid Arab horse, rode on to the wharf. As he reined in, a brown-skinned servant wearing a white turban appeared from nowhere and

28

scuttled down the gangway to take the bridle. The three boys looked nervously at one another.

"We'll speak for ye, laddies," said Dugald kindly. "He'll maybe look for a few white Christians amang all those heathen Hindus. And I can tell him truly ye were awful good with those donkeys."

4

Goodbye, Sydney

NEARLY frantic with anxiety, Mrs Small sat watching from the window. If all three boys were lost, how could she call on the police for help? She herself was nothing but a fugitive, running away from her lawful husband!

It was quite dark when they returned. Jim and Emma were already asleep; but everyone else was in the parlour, waiting for the explanation, which had to be a good one – or it would be the stick for all three.

"We've got donkeys," said Archie.

"Remember that ship we told you about, the *Armenian*?" said Jack.

"He's a judge from India and he's famous," said Bill.

When the story was disentangled there was no stick for the

boys – only amazement and joy. There was a passage on this chartered ship, the *Armenian*! And more than that, there was work, both on the voyage and when they arrived in New Zealand.

"New Zealand!" Mrs Small repeated the name warmly. This was what she had really hoped for – a country more like England, without the harsh dryness of New South Wales.

"We've got to travel in the steerage, and they've got Indians, but they won't hurt us. They're black men but not like our blacks," said Jack.

"They look at us like this," said Archie, turning his eyes from side to side without moving his head.

"And where do *we* travel?" asked Mrs Small.

The three went silent. There was a blow to deliver. Archie and Jack looked at Bill, and Bill screwed up his courage.

"There's a tiny cabin with a berth big enough for Emma to sleep with you."

"But we need another berth."

"That's all the places there are," said Bill, twisting his toes on the carpet.

Mary Ann rose and ran from the room. It was all too plain. There was no passage for her! She lay on her bed with the crocheted cover and pulled the pillow over her ears, and did not move until Mrs McCracken came in to put a comforting arm around her shoulders.

"What are they saying?" she whispered.

"Your mother won't go without you," said Mrs McCracken kindly.

"She must, she must!" Mary Ann sat upright. "How can she stay? There isn't any other ship!"

"I know that, my dear. She says she will go to the judge and plead with him to find room, or she will not go at all. It doesn't seem a hopeful prospect, but your mother is very good at speaking up for what she must have."

"No! Oh, Mrs McCracken, you heard what Bill said – they've seen all over the ship, and there isn't a place; and Mr Cracroft Wilson is such an important gentleman. It's because he *needs* the boys that they can go; and he doesn't need *me*! What can we do?"

"You could stay here with me, and I will keep your passage money, and Mr McCracken will put your name on the list for a ship."

"But if Father should find me!"

"Sydney is a big city. He could look for a long time without finding you; and then, when you must go out, Mr McCracken would go with you."

Mary Ann twisted her handkerchief in her fingers, over and over. At last she said quietly: "Do you think I might find a situation? I can cook very well, I think, and keep house neatly; and I should like some money of my own."

"Now, that's a splendid idea! You could buy yourself some pretty things. Mr McCracken could recommend you to one of his clients at the bank. Will you go and tell them? Or shall I?"

"You go, please, Mrs McCracken."

It was easy to be brave, with only the two of them in the quiet bedroom – but out there, looking into the face of the mother she had never been away from in all her life, it might be different. Mary Ann watched the door close; then she went to the window and drew aside the curtain.

Over the hillsides were scattered the lights of a hundred

lamps. Ships' lanterns gleamed faintly over the harbour; and along her own street moved the bright lights of a carriage. And ever since they had emigrated to Australia she had seen nothing at night but the moon and the stars and the dark shapes of the trees.

The great city! Bent all day over the table and the sewing-machine, and not daring to go into the street for fear that her father should come, she had seen hardly anything of it. Only the handbills for the theatre and the travelling circus, the spires of the churches, and rumours of a library with thousands of books!

"If I must stay, I'll make the most of my chances," Mary Ann vowed to herself.

The door opened and Mrs Small came in, smiling, to give her a warm hug for her courage.

Back in the parlour, there was another serious question to be asked.

"Think carefully, boys," said Mrs Small. "When you were asked your names, what did you say?"

"Bill, of course!"

"Jack."

"Archie!"

"And – Small?"

"I don't think we did. Did we, Jack?"

"They didn't ask our second names."

Mrs Small looked pleased.

"We must have a guardian angel, I think! It would be so easy to name yourselves."

"But why shouldn't we, Mother?"

"Because from now on we are not Smalls. We shall have a

new name that your father won't know, so that he can't ask where we are. I am going to be Mrs Phipps."

"Then I'll be – Bill *Phipps*!"

Bill said his new name slowly, as if he were tasting a new kind of cake; then he grinned, as if it tasted good. He shook hands all round.

"How d'ye do, Jack Phipps! Pleased to meet you, Archie Phipps!"

"Am I *really* Archie Phipps, Mother?"

She ruffled his hair and drew him closer. "It's a game of 'Pretend'. Don't you think it's a nice name to choose?"

"No," said Archie.

"Wait till I tell you a story," she said. "When I was a girl in London, I had a playmate named Lavinia Phipps. Her mother was dead and her father was very poor; and one day he stole a dress for her, because she hadn't anything decent to wear. He was caught and put in prison and sentenced to be transported to Tasmania. But on the way to the ship he managed to jump out of the cart and run away. The people in our street hid him until he could take Lavinia and go to work in Manchester."

"Did Lavinia keep the dress?" asked Archie.

"No, but I helped your grandmother to make her another one. And they never found Mr Phipps or Lavinia; so I think it's a lucky name, and now you must all practise remembering it."

So a game was invented, and played all the time during their last day in Sydney. Whatever anyone might be doing, another could interrupt with a question – like Bill pretending to be the coach-driver asking for the full names of his passengers and they had to answer: "Jack Phipps. Archie Phipps." Mrs McCracken kept a scoreboard with a tick for every time they said *Phipps* and a cross for every time they said *Small*, until nobody was scoring any crosses. As for Emma, her mother made her a special song.

> What's your name? Emma Phipps,
> Peach stones and orange pips
> Kiss the lips of Emma Phipps.

Emma could not sing more than the first line, but she had the "Emma Phipps" part right.

After one more day, when the horses were loaded and the ladies and gentlemen in their cabins, the *Armenian* was ready to sail. At dawn the Phipps family went down with Mr McCracken to help with the boxes on a hired dray; and Mary Ann, not a bit stern, hugged and kissed them all as they left the house, and sat by the window to watch the harbour.

The *Armenian* used all her sixty horse-power to move out from the wharves, while the Phipps children, although longing to look, had to stay below decks. But now in the open waters the sails were set to catch the westerly breeze; and Jack and Jim crept out. Jim was quite fit now, apart from a haze in his mind about how he came to be here when he could not even remember leaving Berrima. A young sailor busy with the ropes looked over in a matey sort of way.

"Ahoy there, shipmate, and what do they call you, now?"

"Jim Small," said Jim promptly.

Jack could have clouted him, but he had to think fast; and to his own surprise the words came smoothly out.

"Isn't he funny? He gets his nickname the wrong way round! We call him *Small Jim*. Small Jim Phipps."

Jack finished up with a good laugh, so that Jim could not help laughing too, till he nearly lost his balance with the rolling of the ship.

"Look to your sea-legs, shipmate, or you'll spend your voyage sitting down," teased the young sailor. And with a stride that seemed to roll with the *Armenian*'s motion, he passed on to his next task, taking no further notice of Small Jim Phipps.

5

Cashmere

THIS was Mr Cracroft Wilson's second journey to New Zealand. He had come four years earlier, when on leave from his duties as a judge, and bought a sheep-run to which he gave an Indian name: Cashmere.

On his first ship, the *Akbar*, he had brought a real menagerie of animals, including antelopes, peacocks and partridges, for he looked forward to hunting as well as farming. But except for some of the peacocks they had all died, and this time he had brought from India only two hares in a cage, and an Indian ass – a pale-looking fellow with a dark stripe running right down his back from his mane to his tail. The poor "jackass" shivered in his pen and Archie had to spend much time soothing him.

The voyage was a fast one, taking only nine days, mostly under full sail but with the engine in use one day when the wind fell. The Phipps family kept to themselves. Mr Cracroft Wilson and his cabin passengers were too grand, and the Indian servants too strange, for these Australian stockmen. This did not trouble Mrs Phipps, who had asked for nothing more than somewhere to go.

She had agreed that they would work at Cashmere for six months – the older boys and herself. Cashmere was short of labour. One of the main ideas behind the planning of the Canterbury settlement was to bring out the right mixture of masters and workmen; but this had not worked very well, partly because too many of the workmen had gone off to Australia looking for gold. Here, for once, was an Australian family coming in the right direction.

Many people came out to admire the *Armenian* as she sailed up Lyttelton Harbour with a brisk nor'easter filling her sails. To the Phipps family the first glimpse of Lyttelton was just as beautiful. After the bare cliffs at the Heads and the steep brown tussocky hills, they came quite suddenly on to the little port, rather like a tiny copy of Sydney with its houses scattered over the hillsides, a few hotels and stores, two jetties and a number of small boats on the water.

The *Armenian* furled her sails and came slowly alongside under steam. Mr and Mrs Cracroft Wilson were handed ashore and followed by the other cabin passengers, all bound for refreshment at the Mitre Hotel. Next, led by Indian servants in white clothes and turbans, came their splendid horses. This caused quite a stir; but most of the watchers had returned to their work by the time the donkeys were led off by three young boys from Australia; and hardly anyone noticed that strange animal the jackass. Mrs Phipps, Emma and Jim came last of all.

The boys found a place to tether the donkeys and let them graze. The town, which still led Christchurch for size, was quite busy. There were four inns, each with its own stables and stockyards; also shipwrights, saddlers, business offices, and the printing works of the *Lyttelton Times*. Best of all in their eyes was a baker's shop with rolls still warm from the oven, and a dairy with fresh milk and butter and cheese.

In Australia Mr McCracken had teased them about going to the "shivery isles". From the first moment ashore, Jim felt the ground slowly rocking from side to side. With alarm he looked at his mother and brothers, but as they did not seem to be worrying, he held his tongue. Only when they reached the steep streets did the rocking become so bad that he grabbed at his mother's skirt. Big as he was, he was terrified that he would slip and slide right down into the sea, which seemed to rise towards him.

"Jim, don't drag on me so!" exclaimed Mrs Phipps.

Jim's eyes grew wide and scary.

"I've *got* to hold on! The earthquake's going to throw me over!"

"Earthquake? There isn't any earthquake!"

"There *is*!" screamed Jim, and he let go and lurched right into the clay of the road.

Jack sprang out to catch him before he could be hurt by the wheel of a dray going past. "It's the waves, stupid! You can feel them rocking still."

"Come, we'll sit down till it goes off," said Mrs Phipps kindly; and they found a bench outside the Canterbury Hotel, where Jim turned his face to the wall to hide his confusion.

Here they were found by a shepherd from Cashmere who had come to show them the way.

This part of the journey was straightforward but slow. Most of their things were packed on to the donkeys, with room on the quietest one for Emma to ride. As for the others, they must walk. The donkeys were in no hurry, but the jackass, which nature had intended for a fast-running animal, took quite a lot of holding. Like all pioneers they climbed the Bridle Path which crossed the hills to the plains.

At every pause there was an enchanting view of the harbour. It was like a long arm reaching from the sea, with three fingers outstretched at the end, and Quail Island humped up in the middle with steep cliffs and a crown of tussock. Most of the highest hills were topped by rocky crags, with Mount Herbert the craggiest and highest of them all, rising above the southern shore.

The family rested at the top of the Bridle Path while the donkeys nosed about among the tussock. Below, for mile after mile the plains stretched out towards the foot of the snowy ranges. They looked bare and dull. The new town of Christ-church in the distance showed only a few buildings dotted among the flax and cabbage trees and patches of swamp. Two small ships were sailing across the estuary of the Avon and Heathcote Rivers; and in the distance the great Waimakariri River shone silver.

After Berrima, which had always been colourful with its oranges and gum-blossom, its bottlebrush and rolling pastures, Christchurch was desolate. Mrs Phipps looked back at the blue water where the *Armenian* lay, very small in the distance, against the wharf; and at the green patches around the bays where grass or crops had been planted.

"I'd sooner be there," she said, "on a sunny slope, with the breeze coming in from the sea!"

But they had to go down the hills to the Heathcote River, and, missing Christchurch out entirely, follow along the edge of the plains to a lonely valley and a few station-buildings scattered around – Cashmere, which meant employment, and a roof over their heads.

It was not really much of a roof, although in those times a station-hand would be lucky to find anything better. They were taken to a big, draughty barracks, with rough bunks slung with sacking, and given a meal of mutton and potatoes. Dusk had set in before the donkeys and the jackass were safely housed in a barn. They could not be left out in the chilly southern evening after coming from Australia; but for their attendants there was neither fire nor light.

The cook was an Indian who had come with Mr Cracroft Wilson on his first journey. He had a way of coming and going among the bare walls and the shadows in perfect silence. This was too much for Emma, who had been beautifully behaved on board ship. She stood by her bunk and screamed. Nothing would make her stay in it: she wanted to jump out, to run and find her own cot which had been left behind at Berrima.

"Cot, cot!" she cried.

When all other soothing failed, Mrs Phipps had a regular answer: to sing. Now, tired out as she was herself, she laid the rag doll Bibi in the bunk and sang to it:

"Up and down the city road
And into the Weasel;
That is how the money's spent,
POP goes the weasel!"

The "POP" was said with a comical face and soon the screams died away and Emma was singing to Bibi, too. Then Mrs Phipps took Emma in her arms and rocked her, still singing, until Emma had no "POP" left in her, for she was fast asleep.

The next morning work began. It had nothing to do with the donkeys or the jackass, which to Archie's great disappointment were left in the barn. They were cutting the tough, stiff blades of the flax. The fertile, sunny valleys were heavy swamp where the flax grew tall enough to hide a horse and his rider. Before they could be drained, ploughed and sown with grass, the leaves must be cut by hand, tied in bundles and rafted down the Heathcote River to a mill.

Mrs Phipps, Bill, Jack and Archie were kept busy while Jim had to take care of Emma. It was not much fun in the swamp. The children soon grew tired of playing hide-and-seek, or of trying to catch the bright blue pukekos who stalked all over the place. But they could not be left at the barracks either, for Emma was afraid of it even in daylight, and the farmhands chased them away from the barns and the stables.

Cashmere was a cruel disappointment. Backs were sore, arms were sore, hands were blistered, and Jack's bruised shoulder began to ache all over again. Bill grumbled that the goldfields could not possibly be worse. Mrs Phipps encouraged them by saying cheerfully that in six months the contract would be finished, with enough money to begin a home; but at nights, lying on her bunk, she calculated that with wages so low it would be more likely to take five years of saving.

What troubled her most was that she could not watch the children properly. When in the second week Emma began waking with nightmares, she decided that it was time to talk to Mr Cracroft Wilson, "The Nabob" as people called him in this little domain which he ruled with all the dignity of an Indian prince.

As it happened, before she could seek him out, "The Nabob" came looking for her. He was very angry, for his overseer had been thrown from his horse and had put the blame on Jim shouting around the stable-yard and causing the animal to shy.

"You must keep your children under better control, Mrs Phipps!" he stormed.

She seized her opportunity.

"I do my best, sir, but this is no place for children."

"What would you have? A nursery?" he said loftily.

"No! I would have work and quarters more suited to my training, where I could look after them properly."

"I don't need any more cooks or house servants. My Indians do very well."

"I'm an expert with a garden, sir; flowers, fruit and vege-tables, and poultry. I don't wish to break my contract. I only wish to be more useful and to give my children a respectable home."

"A garden?" he said.

Mr Cracroft Wilson was thinking: this woman isn't of much use, it's the boys I need; the children are better out of it. He looked over towards the hills.

"There's a place over the Saddle there, I believe, that belongs to me. Sixty-eight acres of land and nearly all of it rough. Two of my men put up a cob cottage and planted some potatoes – and then cleared out to the Australian diggings. I can't spare any more men, so if one room and a chimney will do you, you're welcome to try."

One room and a chimney! Well, that was enough to begin

with, thought Mrs Phipps; she could make a home out of that.

"Is it near the harbour?" she asked.

"Yes. Governors Bay: some seven miles, I believe. It's hardly worth my looking at – you must take my overseer's word for it."

"And I may take all the children?"

"The *children*, Mrs Phipps. The two grown boys, Bill and Jack, will remain here to fulfil their contract."

She saw that she must move carefully now. "I must talk to them," she said. "If they're agreeable, your offer suits me very well, sir."

"You must talk to them!" Mr Cracroft Wilson exploded. "I must remind you, there's a contract that they work for me! That was the condition for your boarding the *Armenian*!"

"We don't break our word. But, sir, you must see that a contract has two sides, and I'll be too far away myself to see to their needs. I ask for your word that they'll be well fed, and clothed, and housed."

The Nabob's eyes flashed. No employee ever told *him* what he must do; but he had his own dignity to keep.

"They are already fed and housed," he said.

"They'll need warm work clothes, with the winter coming," said Mrs Phipps calmly.

"I offer you a house and you try to exact fresh conditions!"

"I'm grateful for your offer, sir, please believe me. But I'm a widow woman and I must leave behind the best hands in my family. I must leave my boys here without protection except from you. You're a man of honour, I know it; give me that promise, and never fear, you won't regret the bargain! Your wilderness will be made to blossom for you."

44

Angry as he was, the Nabob knew that this was good sense.

"Very well," he said. "Your boys shall have what is needful. When the six months have expired, we'll look into the position again. You can take that place over there as *your* cottage. But don't forget – it's *my* property!"

6

Over the Hills

ON a May morning, when the sting of frost was in the air, the Phipps family set out over the hills to Governors Bay.

There was an old track, the Cashmere shepherds told them, where the men who built the cottage used to come to and fro. They were to go up the valley through the flax, then strike up on to the spur to their left and continue on to the Saddle, from which there was a steep descent to the Bay.

With a great many things to be carried, Bill and Jack were allowed two days off to see their mother safely settled. Each of them had a roll of blankets to sling across his back. The pans and dishes were taken out of the wooden trunk and tied into sacks, while the clothes were left in the carpet-bags. These

bundles would have to be slung between two carriers and taken
for short distances, while some of the family came back for
second burdens. However, the distance did not seem very
long – seven or eight miles – and they had a whole day before
them.

"Am I to have a bag of my own?" asked Jim, full of
excitement.

"I shall make you a Dick Whittington bundle," said his
mother.

Mrs Phipps folded her brown shawl into a small square,
placed Jim's clothes in the centre and knotted the corners over
the fork of a smooth stick. Jim poked his koala bear in so that
it looked out of the top, shouldered the bundle gaily and
marched up and down the barracks singing:

> "Turn again Whittington,
> Lord Mayor of London – don – don,
> Ding dong ding dong."

"Turn again!" teased Archie. "You won't get over the top
if you keep turning back!"

"We must make new words," said Mrs Phipps. "How will
this be?

> "Go ahead Whittington
> Over to Lyttelton,
> Find you a home!"

"It isn't Lyttelton, it's Governors Bay," said Jack. "We
should sing, 'Halfway to Lyttelton'."

"Ding dong ding dong," chimed Emma, who liked that
line of the song too well to part with it. She shouldered her rag
doll Bibi and marched around too, to show that she carried
her share.

They set off, still singing cheerfully. Before reaching the flax they could see well up the valley to the Saddle, with the beginning of its dark edging of bush, and the big hill called the Sugarloaf to the left of it. It all looked very clear and simple; and never having been in the New Zealand bush, they imagined it would be like Australia, where there was plenty of space between the trees.

All went well until the track through the flax began to break up into three or four paths and nobody could say which was the proper one. There were no footprints or hoofmarks, nothing but the long leaves and tall flower-stalks that grew so fast as to cover up the marks of men completely.

"Let's take the path that gets us out the quickest," said Bill.

Up above them were the shining leaves of small trees, whiteywood and broadleaf and five-finger. But between this and the flax there lay a belt of creeper throwing out long trailing branches. "Mumma, mumma!" cried Emma. "Ear scratch!"

Ugly spines curved beneath each leaf and along the stalks. Mrs Phipps gently eased the creeper away, but a small trickle of blood went on oozing from the ear-lobe.

"This will be the bush-lawyer they talk of," she said. "Once it gets its grip on you it never lets you go!"

There was no dodging it. They went up and down alongside the mass of bush-lawyer looking for stepping-stones, as if it were a river. And when they found them, Jim and Emma had to be lifted over from hand to hand. Mrs Phipps came last; but she slipped off a leaning rock and the lawyer gripped her up to the knees.

"Mumma, Mumma!" wailed Emma in terror. But Mrs Phipps began to laugh, so that Emma had to laugh too, and her mother seemed not to notice how her own hands bled as she eased the spines from her dress.

The scrub was not easy to walk through either. It was gay with fantails flitting and swooping everywhere, and bellbirds singing as they searched for late berries; and this would have been delightful but for the supplejack vines, which made such a tangle that Jack had to cut a track with his sheath-knife. "We must go upwards to the tussock-grass," said Mrs Phipps; but when they tried this, they came to a rocky bluff impossible to climb.

"We could edge along it till there's a place to go up," said Jack.

"Or work back," said Bill.

So Mrs Phipps had to wait while both ways were explored and listen to the shouting of arguments as to which way was the best. In the end they followed Jack; and his way turned out to be almost directly upwards, hand over hand, with only roots and small bushes to hold on to. It was a great trial passing the bundles up; and worse than the bundles was Emma, for she whimpered with fright and refused to move, and had to be dragged. Then Jim almost lost his grip from sneezing as the spores of the ferns got into his nose. To cap everything, when at last they sat down on a patch of level grass, right under their eyes was Bill's chosen way – an easy slope. This was too much for Bill.

"You idiot!" he shouted.

He let fly a punch at Jack's chest and bowled him over. Jack bounded back like a boomerang and the next minute was on top of Bill, pummelling him. "Stop, stop!" yelled Archie, trying to get in between the flying feet and taking a kick from each brother for his trouble. That was the end of it. Mrs

Phipps stood over them with a stick in her hand; a rough pronged stick.

"Get up both of you if you don't want the sharp edge of this! Do you want to be sent directly back to Cashmere? Isn't *one* baby enough to carry?" Suddenly she smiled. "Blows are a poor answer when stomachs call for food. There's bread and cheese and a patch of sunshine – time for a spell!"

The sunshine was cosy and Jim began singing as he set down his bundle:

"Go ahead Whittington,
Halfway to Lyttelton,
Find you a home –
Ding dong ding dong,"

so that weary Emma fell fast asleep in her mother's lap, with the half-eaten bread in her hand. Archie and Jim and Jack wandered around the tussock while Bill sat staring moodily over the plains, nursing his anger.

When Emma woke they walked steadily up the long steep slope. Now she rode pick-a-back with Bill, while the others managed the bundles, which had to be lifted and carried and dropped and left and returned for over and over again. There was much circling around clumps of matagouri which were all thorn, and Archie had his first taste of a Spaniard, which looked like another tussock until he stepped on its cruel spines. "I never knew there were so many prickly things in this country," said Mrs Phipps.

It was afternoon before they reached the Saddle. Then, for one glorious moment, the long grind of the climb was quite forgotten in the picture spread before them – the upper harbour with its three long fingers separated by chains of low hills, Quail Island right in the centre, Mount Herbert rising square beyond and the water dreaming and blue. All this they saw over the tops of the bush which hid the shoreline of Governors Bay.

Jim burst out singing again:

> "Go ahead Whittington,
> Halfway to Lyttelton,
> Find you a home –"

"Ding dong ding dong!" chimed Emma. "Ding dong ding dong!"

Jack was looking at something even more inviting than the harbour – a narrow gully which reached down from the tall Sugarloaf hill to the left of them. Surely this meant a stream; and they were all dreadfully thirsty, for they had found nothing on the way up but a small trickle oozing beneath a rock.

He led the way down into the bush. But this was the southerly and shaded face of the hills, a wet mass of rocks and logs and ferns and supplejacks; so that it was a long time before the gully levelled slightly and water could be seen shining under a thicket of soft green bushes. Emma slid from Bill's back and put out her hand for a drink. Next moment she was screaming:

"Mumma, mumma, it bit me!"

"Little goose! It bit you – did it?" Bill couldn't resist a laugh, but the smile on his face quickly straightened when it "bit" him, too. His hand felt as if tiny red-hot needles had been driven into the palm; and with the screen of leaves in the way he could not even cool it in the water.

"Keep away! It must be a nettle," said Mrs Phipps, eyeing the downy hairs that clung to the stalks.

This was more easily said than done. The nettle grew thickly all down the gully, which had to be skirted for some distance before they spied a pool that was free of it. By this time Bill's hand was numb, and the water did not take away the sting; but at least it was wonderful to drink the dark marshy water.

"We must make for the ridge, where it's too dry for the nettle," said Mrs Phipps.

They worked over to the ridge on their left, only to find that it ended in a bluff. At least from here there was some sort of a view; and it seemed that more bluffs extended in that direction, while the spur on the right had an even slope. But to reach it meant re-crossing the gully and finding another way through the nettles! They were considering this daunting prospect when Jim discovered that his Dick Whittington bundle had gone.

"My koala! My koala!" he wailed.

"Your koala! All your clothes are in that bundle," said his mother sharply.

"Where did you drop it?" demanded Bill.

"Did you put it down to have a drink?" Jack added.

Jim had no idea, but only sat sobbing for his lost koala.

"You must all go and look," said Mrs Phipps firmly to the boys.

"Let *him* look," growled Jack. "I'd like to spank him, I would."

"How could we find it?" said Archie in a low voice.

Since leaving the Saddle he had said hardly anything, and now he looked up with eyes like a beaten puppy's – almost exhausted.

"If we *could* find it, Mother," said Bill sensibly, "how would we find *you* again?"

Mrs Phipps considered this for a moment, and looked at Archie's weary face, and listened to Jim's sobs, with the addition now of a frightened whimper from Emma.

"We will all go together," she said gently.

"Let me go first," said Jack. "I'll find the places where I cut the supplejack. It'll be easy!"

But it was not easy. Everything looked different from the opposite direction, and the children kept arguing wearily whether they had passed this stump, or that stone, making wrong turns and having to come back again. Only the knife-cuts were a sure guide; and in the end they did come back to the drinking-pool, to see the bundle sitting safely on a stone, with the koala's head peeping jauntily out. This cheered everyone a little, and also they were ready for another drink of water.

> "Go ahead Whittington,
> Halfway to Lyttelton,
> Find you a home—"

sang Mrs Phipps. Nobody else joined in; not even Jim. He would sooner have lain down to sleep.

They worked across to the spur on the right, slowly descending. The birds were out for their afternoon feeding. On the ground there were saddlebacks and a pair of the orange-wattled crow, while friendly tomtits and brown bush-robins chattered from the low branches, to cheer Archie up and to make Emma laugh. It seemed now that only a short distance remained, as the bush dwindled and they came out into a patch of bracken fern.

Low-growing at first, the fern became a little taller as they went on, and unexpectedly they found themselves surrounded by wiry stalks that reached right above their heads.

"Let me go first and smash it down," said Bill.

The numbness in his hand was wearing off, but still it was easier to use his elbows. Soon he had to do more – to fling his whole length forward and open a path. Again and again he did this, and when he grew tired, Jack took a turn. They inched their way along, dragging or passing their bundles and bags along the narrow track, scraping their skin and leaving more tatters on their clothes than they dared to notice. To fall on the springy fern was to want to lie there and sleep – but the sun was already cut off by the hills, and the chill of the coming night was sharp on their faces. Archie was silent; Jim was sneezing from the dust; and Emma clung so tightly to her mother's arms that her fingers went white. They had no idea whether they were going deeper into the fern or coming out of it, or in which direction they ought to go.

"Mother," whispered Jack, "what shall we do if we can't get out?"

This was the very question she was asking herself; but she would not alarm anyone by admitting it. "We shall go on till we do," she whispered back; and then loudly, in a cheery voice: "Shall we stop a while, and see what's left in the lunch bag?"

A small nest was rolled in the fern and the billy opened for its bread and cheese. Archie took a bite on the dry cheese and broke his silence.

"I can't eat it! I'm thirsty. I want a drink."

"D'ink, d'ink!" cried Emma.

"Soon there'll be water. Here's bread, Emma!"

"I'm cold," she whimpered.

"Ugh, yes! It gives me the shivers," said Jack.

Mrs Phipps rounded on him, speaking softly but bluntly:

"You boys must say nothing about your discomforts, nothing at all, do you hear? Can't you see how they will begin, the little ones? We must keep our courage up! The fern won't go on for ever and then there's a home – somewhere to put your foot down!"

Bill said nothing. He munched his food until the gnawing inside him went away;. then he began again to smash down a path. He came at once to a sort of bank densely covered with another growth – tutu. How would they get through that, and if they did, where would it lead? Try this way or that, it was a hopeless puzzle. Overhead the sky was quite grey, and all their hands were now stiff with cold.

Perhaps this is the moment, thought Mrs Phipps, in spite of all her determination, when we must bed ourselves down, thirsty and cold as we are...

Suddenly out of the silence came a long, strong sound:

"Ah – oo! Ah – oo!"

"It's a cow!" cried Archie, with the joy of one meeting an old friend. "It's a cow!"

"Where there's a cow, there's a farm," said Mrs Phipps. "Come, we'll call."

One – two – three! At the tops of their voices they yelled together, "Coo-ee! Coo-ee!"

Silence. Not even the cow. Only the first owl from the hillside answered, "Morepork. Morepork!"

"Again. *Coo-ee.* COO-EEE!"

Quite near, but lifted up, a man's voice shouted:

"Who's there? Where a-a-are you?"

"Here. HERE!"

To and fro they called, giving their position, receiving directions: back there, to the left here, yes, that'll be right.

Then there was a bank miraculously clear of the fern and the tutu, a man's figure standing on it dark against the sky, two hands outstretched to lift Emma from her mother's arms and to hand the five others up, one by one. To the friendly voice was now added the friendly face of a young man.

"Well! What a time you've had! But you're safe in Governors Bay. And allow me to introduce myself: I'm John Dyer."

"We're much obliged, Mr Dyer. And we are the Phipps family. We're looking for a cob hut that's been left empty."

"Belonging to Nabob Wilson?"

"Yes."

"Oh! That's not far away."

"Hurrah! Hurrah!" shouted Jack, and he spun round on his toes for the sheer joy of it. "Hurrah!" cried Bill.

"I want a drink," said Archie.

"Do you, young fellow? How about fresh milk and hot cocoa? Leave your things here: we'll go down to my house."

He hoisted Archie on to his back and strode off down his familiar path. Jim clung tight to his Dick Whittington bundle and tried to sing; but somehow the tune had come unstuck from the words. As for Emma, she lay across her mother's shoulder as if she were already asleep; but the next moment she jerked upright and pointed.

"Look, look!"

It was the most beautiful sight in all the world: a candle shining in a window.

7

A Place to Put Your Foot Down

AN hour later there came from John Dyer's cottage a procession of people, every one of them filled to the brim with food, warmth and friendliness. The light of a storm-lantern made queer-looking patches on the trees; and the familiar scent of young blue-gums mingled with the unfamiliar scent of seaweed from the near-by shore. First went Mr Dyer, leading a pack-bullock with the blanket-rolls strapped to its back. Next came the boys, putting down tired legs one after the other, stiffly, like toy soldiers. Emma was fast asleep in her mother's arms. Last of all came a large collie dog.

"I doubt if you'll find the place in much condition for living,

Mrs Phipps," Mr Dyer had said, "for it's been long neglected."

"I'll make a home of it, so long as it's mine to try," she
answered smiling, and thinking of the barracks at Cashmere
which were beyond anything she could do.

Now they passed beneath some more trees and into a clearing
– and there in the moonlight stood the white walls, bare and
lonely. "Hurrah!" cried Jack, running forward, but Mr Dyer
called him back.

"Wait," he said. "There's sure to be rats, and the rats could
be fierce. If you're wise, you'll let Ranger go first."

"Rats!" echoed Archie with a shudder – they were the only
animals he had ever hated.

The door opened with a heavy scraping. The collie did not
hesitate for a moment. With short barks and loud snufflings
he worked rapidly about the shadowy walls, while the family
propped one another up, shivering. At last he trotted quietly
out. The rats had escaped through a dozen holes, but they had
been scared out of their wits.

Everyone crowded inside and the lantern-light played on the
fireplace, the boxes scattered around, the two rough bunks,
the litter on the floor. The window was only a square hole
covered with glazed calico. The place stank of musty wood,
rotting potatoes and the recently-departed rats. The boys
shrank back to the cool, sweet air in the doorway – but Mrs
Phipps only handed the sleeping Emma to Mr Dyer and seized
the manuka broom which leaned against the mantelpiece.

"All we need for tonight is a patch of clean ground," she
said. "We won't need rocking to put us to sleep, and tomorrow we can put our backs into it. You won't know it for
the same place."

In one long line, fully dressed, with blankets above and below and folded under the heads, the Phipps family lay down. Comfortingly, the lantern was left on the mantelpiece. "I can find my way back blindfold," said Mr Dyer, cheerfully wishing them good night. Emma and Jim slept in the middle of the line. Because of the rats, Mrs Phipps kept a stout stick beside her, alongside the wall; and Jack with his sheath-knife handy was next to the door. But even this fear could not keep them awake for five minutes; and fortunately the collie had done his work well.

Not rats, but a bar of sunlight woke Jack in the morning. He edged away from the sleeping Archie and stepped outside. Every piece of him ached with stiffness and his shoulder reminded him of its old bruises. He moved out into the centre of the clearing and looked around at its encircling trees, at the Sugarloaf towering above, and at Mount Herbert with it squared-off crags, like the Egyptian Sphinx he had seen in a book; and a joyful thought came surging up inside him.

Father will never find us here!

Mr Dyer had left a water-bottle beside the doorway. Jack took a drink, stretched himself fully awake, and began to explore.

The clearing was almost square, sloping gently to the beginning of the fern, where it was steep. On two sides there was a belt of small trees, and on the verge of what must be the stream that flowed from the Sugarloaf was a mass of flax, tutu and tall toetoe grass with swaying golden plumes.

Jack mounted the slope to get a view of the harbour. It gleamed like glass, except where it was rippled by a dinghy with a single oarsman rocking to and fro. By the time it had passed out of sight, Jack had formed his great ambition.

A boat! *I must have a boat!*

At that moment an angry grunting and snorting burst from the near-by fern. Jack swung round. Glowering at him, with short tusks showing under its quivering snout, was a great hairy iron-grey pig. Jack's hand went to his hip, and found nothing; his sheath-knife was still lying on the floor of the cottage. He glared back at the boar – and the boar grunted again and disappeared.

Jack raced back down the slope. In the doorway stood Emma rubbing her eyes; everyone else was still fast asleep. He slipped quietly inside and buckled on his sheath-knife; then he took Emma by the hand and set out to explore in the other direction.

In the bush that lined the shore, the bellbirds were singing loudly while two woodpigeons, stuffed fat with fuchsia berries, sat lazily on a branch. A track sloped towards the beach. Emma ran ahead with shouts of joy and danced on the sand. Shells were piled in ridges just beyond the tide – she picked them up by handfuls and flung them far and wide. When she came to the little stream trickling into the sea, she felt it with her bare toes, gasped "Ooh!" and splashed on.

"Ooh!" she cried again, in a voice high with excitement. "Chook! Chook!"

Two brown birds like overgrown chickens stalked out of the bushes to peck around among the dry seaweed. Emma fussed about trying to catch them, but the wekas did not mind in the least, as they were always a few steps ahead. Jack's eyes were turned to the harbour, watching the circles where the fish had leaped – they would really be worth the catching! He wondered where the boat had gone. Then he heard Emma.

"Ooble, ooble, water bubble; ooble, ooble, water bubble," she sang.

Yes! Water was bubbling, sure enough, right where she was sitting on a green bank above the sand. Jack lifted her down and she stopped singing long enough to say "Ooh! Cold!" and shake out the wet hem of her dress. She reached out her hands again to catch the "bubble" – a clear, delicious spring tumbling out into a hollow which someone had smoothed to hold a billy or a pannikin. Sedges reached across the little pool since its makers had left.

"Come, Emma – let's tell Mother we've found fresh water!"

"Ooble, ooble, water bubble," sang Emma all the way up the beach.

They found Mrs Phipps, with her long sandy hair already brushed and twisted into a bun, busy laying an outdoor fire. "I can't test the chimney until everyone is up," she said, "and if they're still asleep on that hard ground, it's sleep they need."

The day was solid work. Water was carried and a tripod built over the fire. Mr Dyer came early with his pack-bullock, bearing all the remaining bundles, an axe and a spade, and a billy of beautiful fresh milk.

"You must come to me if you're short of anything you need," he said, "or to the other cottage – I'll show the lad where to find it."

"I'm Jack," said the lad promptly.

"I beg your pardon, Jack! I couldn't sort you all out last night. About the next cottage: that's where Mrs Parsons lives. She's my sister. And Charles Parsons shares the farm with me. I don't doubt we'll all be good neighbours."

"We're much obliged to you, Mr Dyer," said Mrs Phipps. "I trust we shall be the same."

"Can I go with Mr Dyer now?" asked Jack eagerly.

"And no breakfast?"

"I'll soon be back!" he promised.

Mrs Phipps made hot bread-and-milk in the billy, and Jack, true to his word, was home before his sleepy brothers had finished eating.

It was time to examine the hut. There was a partition at one end which had appeared, in the lamplight, to be the end wall. In that tiny bedroom was a second calico window and two more bunks, made of nothing better than forked stakes driven into the ground to support saplings and a mesh of small branches. The sacking which covered them was chewed by the rats, and the mesh was broken in many places.

The open fireplace took up all one end of the kitchen, with chains and hooks for the billies and iron bars on which to rest the pans. There was no furniture except for boxes and packing-cases. "All the quicker for the cleaning," said Mrs Phipps. She had everyone running in and out until the hut was quite bare and all the litter swept up into the fireplace. Dry twigs were piled on top, the fire was lit, the green leaves were thrown on the blaze to make plenty of smoke. Mrs Phipps and the boys watched keenly for any wisp of smoke coming out in the wrong places. But no, the high chimney carried it all clear of the thatch.

Small though it was, the hut was completely sound. The rat-holes along the earthen floor had to be stopped up with stones. As for the roof, a few patches of thatch needed renewing, and this had to be done with tussock which was not handy to find; so Jack and Bill, who had thought they were free of flax-cutting, were sent again to the near-by gully to fetch flax and toetoe for temporary repairs.

Archie and Mrs Phipps took out the axe and cut a pile of strong, supple branches to mend the bunks. There was no sacking to be found, but in the gully there was a mass of vine – pohuehue – with dry, springy stalks, which was as good as a wire mattress. The blankets were aired and shaken and laid neatly on top.

Now the boxes were soused in the tide to cleanse them of insects, and dried out in the sunshine before being arranged for table and chairs and shelves. Jack sat cross-legged on the ground plaiting one flax rope after another and enjoying the work. The ropes were slung across and along the room to carry clothes and other belongings, for there were no cupboards or drawers. Pots and pans, cups and plates, all had to be arranged. "A place for everything and everything in its place!" said Mrs Phipps.

In the midst of it all danced Emma, bent on finding the best place for Bibi, but each time the doll had to make way for something else. So Jack made her a tiny flax hammock and hung it in the corner. "Lullabye, bye, bye!" crooned Emma, as she swung the doll in the hammock happily to and fro.

At last Mrs Phipps surveyed the room and could think of only one more thing to be done. She took out her own treasure – the toby-jug that had been a wedding-present.

"Who will find me some flowers? You, Jim?"

"Me, me!" cried Emma. She did not know enough words to explain, but she had seen flowers, down near the spring. Off she ran with Jim after her. Yes, there was a bush covered with purple-pink spikes – the koromiko. Emma was in such a hurry she would have pulled every flower off short if Jim had not been there to make sure of good long stalks.

"Why, it's like a bottlebrush!" said Mrs Phipps, very pleased, "only there's no handle coming out at the end."

She set the toby-jug full of flowers on the window-ledge; and the house became a home.

8

The Robber in the Garden

AFTER lunch, which was of bread and cheese and a drink of milk, Mrs Phipps examined her garden.

Beneath its covering of weeds, the dug ground should be full of potatoes. But what were the bare patches where the ground had been torn up? Had someone been here to rob – Maoris perhaps, who used some digging stick instead of a regular spade? She turned over the patches carefully. Yes, her guess was right: there were no potatoes here. Only where the weeds were undisturbed did she find them, and they were no great crop, even there. There would certainly not be enough to feed them through the winter.

She sat down in the sunshine to rest, feeling disappointed and baffled.

Emma was fast asleep on her new bunk, and Jim and Archie were stretched out on the ground, still weary after yesterday's wanderings and today's hard work. Bill and Jack had gone to Mr Dyer to ask for advice on where they might buy some hens. There was no sign of them yet; and Mrs Phipps got up again and went on to examine the edges of the clearing.

Ah! This was better! There were small fruit trees and berry bushes, well placed for the sun. Creepers were already clambering over them, but half an hour's pulling left the healthy young branches open to the air. Cherries, plums, peaches, gooseberries, and some shrubs that might perhaps be currants.

"I must make a list of tools," she said to herself. "And plants, and seeds. This is warm land that will bring the crops early! Only let us get through the winter, and we shall be prosperous here."

She took the spade again and had turned up a small pile of potatoes, still puzzling, when she heard voices.

"Mother! Mother!" called Bill. "There's a Mrs Dobbs that has pullets. You can get them as soon as the hen run is ready. We saw a lot of houses – how many, Jack?"

"About six!" said Jack. "Mr Parsons goes to Lyttelton in a boat with oars, and a sail. When can we get a boat, Mother?"

"Hold on!" she laughed. "We must get through the winter first. What I want to know is: who has been stealing our potatoes?"

Jack gave a quick glance at the torn patch of earth.

"Wild pigs," he said promptly.

"Pigs!"

"Yes! Mr Dyer said they're real pests, and you're to watch

out, they might go for Emma or Jim. And besides – I *saw* the robber this morning."

Jack told his story, which had somehow been forgotten in all the rush of work.

"So! We must dig the crop at once and remove the temptation," said Mrs Phipps.

"*Now*, Mother? Must we?" pleaded Bill.

She took pity on him. "No – I'll have Archie and Jim help me tomorrow. Today, we'll stack a heap of firewood: all sizes, every kind, and I'll find out which of them burn the best."

The owls were beginning to call "morepork" from the hills when Jack gathered his last armful. Most of the big logs were rotten, but his mother needed good-sized pieces for that great fireplace. When he saw a dry branch twice as thick as his arm sticking out from a shrub, Jack pulled.

He might have been hauling on a bell-rope, so quickly came the noise of rumbling and grunting. For the second time that day Jack found himself face to face with a young boar – *the* boar.

Before Jack could retreat, the boar charged. With a bound, catching at an overhead branch with his good arm, Jack swung himself clear, but there was not enough strength in his other shoulder to haul his body up and he had to let go and race around the tree to climb it from the trunk. He sat astride a branch while his angry enemy scraped and backed about among the leaves below.

Should he call out, and bring Bill running to help him? No! Jack wanted to settle accounts himself with this robber who had tried to beat him down. He had heard talk of pig-hunting among the shepherds at Cashmere and desperately he tried to remember. They used dogs, and he had no dog; but

he took out his sheath-knife and felt the point. The flax-cutting had not blunted it.

Very quietly he began to ease himself along the branch until it drooped beneath his weight. The boar backed. Jack slid farther: the boar moved again. Had the beast come forward and raised his head, he could have reached Jack's ankle; but he stood back, waiting his opportunity. Well then, Jack must be first! He braced himself against a second branch, took a flying leap and landed on top of the boar. Somewhere in the back of his memory he could hear a voice saying: *Take him by the hind leg and turn him over.*

Jack grabbed at the leg and held it tightly. But how was he to turn the boar over, while only his own weight kept the lashing beast under control? Perhaps the boar would get tired first! He held on grimly, grunting like the pig with his own exertion, keeping his left hand on the knife.

Then sharply, suddenly, he rolled off, pulled the boar with him and saw the throat stretched out beneath the snout. He thrust out with all the strength his left arm could muster and drove the point into the skin. The boar gave a violent lurch and kicked him over.

Jack scrambled to his feet and did not wait for more. The pain in his shoulder told him that he would never have the strength to repeat the blow. He ran away from the hideous squealing, back down the slope to the cottage. He must get Bill to come with the axe.

In the glow of the firelight he saw his mother take out the damper she had made for their supper. It was a round of dough shaped like a huge scone, made of flour and salt and water, and cooked on a flat stone among the embers. The damper smelt warm and mellow, but it was poor food after all.

"Grab the axe, Bill, I've caught the robber," shouted Jack.

"The axe?" said Mrs Phipps, startled.

Jack grinned.

"You'll have pork for dinner tomorrow," he said.

9

Crisis at Cashmere

THE next day, Mr Dyer went with the boys to the Saddle and showed them his own way over. With nothing to carry, the walk would take them little more than three hours.

Mrs Phipps had now to harvest the potatoes and work over her land with only Archie and Jim to help. There was little to do in the house, for they could only afford the simplest of meals: porridge and tea and damper and pork and potatoes. Like other settlers she learned to eke out the tea by mixing in dried biddy-bids. She could not bake bread, for she had no yeast and no camp-oven. But one day, while bringing water from the spring, Archie nibbled at a thick green leaf and liked the taste. Mrs Phipps cooked some of the leaves and they did very well instead of spinach.

A fowl-run was built with a log house and a fence of criss-crossed sticks. Into this went the pullets and a big rust-coloured rooster. Tools, plants, seeds, a few supplies, and a wooden tub to be placed before the fire to serve as a bath were bought in Lyttelton. Mr Parsons fetched these things in his boat and landed them on the sandy beach.

Late autumn passed into winter. Storms came, but there were no hard frosts in this sheltered bay. The dug ground lay ready, the fruit trees were trimmed, new ones were planted, and strawberries were set out on a sunny bank. At nights Mrs Phipps sat mending and patching the clothes by the light of the fire and the slush-lamps, which were made from pig's fat set in a tin with a home-made wick in the centre. These winter evenings were jolly; for while she stitched, Mrs Phipps told stories to the children, or sang long ballads with a chorus for them all to join in. After Emma had fallen asleep, or on wet days, their mother took out books and slates and pencils to begin teaching Jim and Archie their letters and numbers.

They knew now that Mr and Mrs Parsons were not only farmers, but school-teachers. That was how they had met and fallen in love – teaching school on the long sea journey from England. In time, the boys would go to school at the Parsons's cottage; but they could wait until Bill and Jack had served their term at Cashmere; and besides, there would be three-pence a day to pay, and lesson-books into the bargain.

Meanwhile Archie and Jim had plenty to learn out-of-doors. With no pet to keep for himself, Archie made friends with the bush birds. He found that a little sugared water in a deep shell would bring the tuis and bellbirds close to the door. Tomtits, fantails and robins hopped around without any enticement at all. The saucy wekas were curious about these odd human beings and even came right into the hut to steal a shiny tea-spoon. As for the slow, stupid and lovable woodpigeons, they were so tame that many a one ended up as a tasty meal for a settler's table.

Archie did not like this idea when he first heard talk of pigeon stew. But when the pork ran out and everyone was growing tired of potatoes and porridge, Mrs Phipps went quietly through the bush with a long pole, until she found an over-fed bird dozing on a low branch. He did not even turn his head as she stunned him and swept him to the ground. That evening, Archie had to harden his heart; and it was not so difficult with that delicious smell coming from the pot.

The boys were hunters on the beach, too. Up at the Pinnacle, a steep rock that stood out of the sea but could be climbed at low tide, there were mussels and rock-oysters, and big red crabs that would grip on a stick to be hauled up. Once, early in the morning, they found stranded on the shore a thin fish that was longer than Archie was tall. It served for three meals. Mr Dyer said it was a frost-fish.

One day, Mrs Parsons came to call. She was a tall, smartly-dressed woman who was fast friends with the children within half an hour. She was delighted to learn that the boys would be her pupils next year, and asked how Bill and Jack were faring.

"They have no means of telling me," said Mrs Phipps. "I should dearly love to see for myself."

"Could I take these three to my house for a day? You'd like to see my picture books, wouldn't you, Jim? And I'll make you some currant buns!"

"I can draw pictures, too," said Jim proudly. He could hardly wait for this special treat.

On the next fine morning they all went to the Parsons's cottage, and Mrs Phipps set off over the Saddle. Mr Dyer's route was easily followed. When she rested it was not because she needed to, but to enjoy the harbour with its blending shades of blue, and the hills with their spurs and gullies and craggy tops. Although it was mid-winter, the sun was warm and the bush was still; but when she came out on to the tussock facing the Plains, with its homesteads and cultivated squares dotted here and there, a cold north-east wind swept up to meet her. Patches of ice and hard frost clung to the shaded hollows.

Mrs Phipps drew her shawl close around her shoulders and hurried on.

When she came to Cashmere, she could find no one about the barracks but the Indian cook who, confused at her arrival and with many gestures to help out his halting English, pointed in the direction of the swamp.

Six weeks earlier she had worked there herself, cutting the flax. Now they were putting in a drain, but meantime the winter ground was more boggy than ever, and icy water squelched over her ankles and oozed into her boots. Soon she saw the knot of workmen – two tall men with strong forks and spades loosening the old roots, and beyond them, half-hidden in the ditch, bare hands grubbing out the clods and hurling them out.

"Bill! Jack! I've come!" she called.

Two short grubbing tools came flying out after the clods, and the boys leapt out of the ditch and came towards her.

The biting wind blew across the swampland to send a great shiver rippling down Jack's shoulders. He wore no jersey, and his bare arm showed through a rip the whole length of his shirt-sleeve. This was the same shirt, the same pair of trousers that he had worn when he left her! Bill was dressed no better, and the bones pressed against the skin of his shoulders. On their bare feet, through the dirty scum left by the swamp water, showed red, ugly lumps – something they had never known in Australia: chilblains.

Mrs Phipps went white with horror and anger.

"What have they done to you?" she cried. She turned to the man with the fork. "Who is responsible for this?"

The man shrugged. "I ain't no boss, lady. And I ain't no nursemaid either."

"We don't do this for pleasure ourselves," said the second man.

Suddenly Jack, forgetting he was a working-man, reached out and took his mother's hands.

"Mother, let us come home!"

"We wanted to run away," said Bill in a low voice, "but they sit watching us at night – and there's the contract, and the wages. We didn't know what to do."

They began to walk away in the direction of the barracks, leaving the labourers standing.

"Who watches you?" demanded Mrs Phipps.

"The Indians."

"The Indians!"

"We're in their quarters now – and we can't eat their food even when there's enough of it!"

"And we work till we're fair beat," said Jack.

"Nabob Wilson allows *this*!" cried Mrs Phipps. "He gave me his promise!"

"We never see him."

"He rode by one day – I tried to stop him but he took no notice," said Bill. "The contract –"

"The contract is broken!" Mrs Phipps said angrily. "He has broken it. They have not kept the promise on which my promise depended. Go in there, boys, and collect your things."

"That won't take long," said Bill bitterly, but he was full of joy at the same time.

The Indian cook came to the doorway and jabbered in broken English so excitedly that it was impossible to understand him. Mrs Phipps only said firmly, "I am going to see the judge. I am going to see Mr Cracroft Wilson." While she stood there the boys collected their bundles and dodged out.

"Have you no boots?" asked Mrs Phipps. "None at all?"

"They have fallen to pieces," answered Jack.

"Then go slowly up the hill, and wait for me."

In spite of their painful feet the boys began running; and the Indian cook, though he would have tried to stop them, was unwilling to push past Mrs Phipps who still blocked the doorway. When she felt sure they were well away she turned and, with a proud step and cold fury inside her, set off for the homestead. She found the Nabob in the stable-yard, grooming his horse.

"Good morning, Mrs Phipps!" he said. "And how have you found Governors Bay? Your boys are working in the swamp, I think; it's being drained."

"No, they're not," she said bluntly. "I've sent them home."

The Nabob gaped.

"*You* have sent them home! Mrs Phipps, they are contracted to work here for six months!"

"The contract is broken, sir. *You* have broken it, not I."

"*I* have broken it?" The nerve of this little woman! "I don't know what you are talking of! I brought you from Australia to work for me."

"You gave me your promise that they would be well fed, and housed, and clothed. I find them starving, shivering, with no boots to their feet, crippled with chilblains and housed with the Indians. I left them sturdy and strong in spirit; and I find them cowed and miserable."

"Where I house my workers is my concern, madam. My Indians are my faithful servants."

"I hold nothing against them, but their ways are strange –"

He interrupted her furiously.

"*You* are not employed here, Mrs Phipps! You will please remove yourself from this property. You are a trespasser, madam!"

"And you have dared to trespass on the self-respect of my boys!" she cried. "I assure you, sir, I have come only to do you the courtesy of informing you of their departure. They have already removed themselves without your invitation."

"You forget yourself! I must remind you that the house where you live is at my disposal. I could turn you off with less warning than you are giving me."

If he thought this would frighten her, he had mistaken his woman.

"You must turn me off in person, then," she said calmly. "But I think you have your own interests too much at heart. I and my family are of more service to you when we are *not* driven. Why don't you come to Governors Bay? You will see a cottage that was falling away from neglect, and a garden that was ruined by the wild pigs, all in perfect order, with young fruit trees already planted. What will you do with it?

Give it to the care of idlers who will run off when the fancy takes them, as your last tenants did?"

The Nabob could hardly believe his ears. No one ever spoke to him in this way! But there was no answering her argument: it would not pay him to turn her out.

"See that your boys are obedient to you, then, if they cannot be obedient to me. I shall come to Governors Bay when it suits my convenience. Go, now!"

She thanked him courteously and hurried away up the hillside. Beyond the plantation of young English trees, out of sight of the homestead and the Nabob and the swamp, she stopped to get her breath, and found herself laughing.

"Not a word said about their wages!" she remembered. "Let him keep what he owes, then. May it comfort him for his loss!"

She went on. It was much easier this way, with the steep climb at the beginning, than the route they had taken on their first nightmare journey over the hills. She had to stop for breath once or twice, and then she saw Bill and Jack waving down to her. They were perched on a rock, sheltered from the cool wind, and rubbing some warmth into their feet; but the warmth only brought the sting into the chilblains.

"Your feet!" said Mrs Phipps. "We must do something about this – you can't go over stones and tussock and heath like that. Let me see inside your bundles."

Inside, neatly folded, were the good jackets and trousers she had bought in Sydney. It had never occurred to either of the boys, cold though they had been every day, to turn them into working clothes. Apart from these there were only ragged singlets and shirts.

Mrs Phipps ripped the old worn shirts into strips and

carefully bound up the sore and grimy feet. As for the good clothes, the boys must put them on at once. They looked very funny indeed – with bags on their feet and smart Sydney jackets on their shoulders – and both boys broke into roars of laughter. Bill took up a stone and sent it bouncing down the hillside for sheer joy; and Jack sent another bouncing down after it.

"I can't believe it's us – and we're free, free, *free*!" cried Bill. The wind carried his voice to echo across the valley: "Fre-e-e!"

It was a wonder that the whole of Governors Bay wasn't roused as the three Phippses came over the Saddle, singing all the way.

10

Maori Challenge

MRS PHIPPS took some of her dwindling store of money and walked into Lyttelton with Archie to buy warm working clothes for Bill and Jack. The clay road, more than six miles long, followed the fringe of the harbour, over spurs and around bays and through patches of bush and of open tussock. Halfway to Lyttelton they passed by the Maori village of Rapaki, but nobody was about.

The boys' feet soon healed and their flesh filled out again with rest, warmth and good food. True, much of the food had to be caught, but Jack was specially good at catching wekas and pigeons, and it was always possible to find shellfish and crabs. There was plenty of work still to be done in readiness for the spring season.

One day, Bill was at work putting a fence along the top of the section when Mr Dyer came looking for straying calves. The upright totara posts, dragged from the bush and pierced with holes at either end, were already in position with long rails fitted into the holes. There was no centre rail and Bill was filling in the space with strong flax sticks, criss-crossed and bound firmly at top and bottom.

Mr Dyer watched Bill's capable hands with admiration. He himself came from a family of English gentleman farmers and had made many blunders while growing used to this rougher kind of life.

"You've a big job there," he said.

Bill pointed to the slope already prepared for the sowing. "We have to keep the pigs off the garden," he said.

"You're making a grand success of it. You must have been born for this life."

"Me, Mr Dyer? Not me! I'd've stayed in Australia and swagged it to the diggings if I could."

"You mightn't have to go to Australia for that, before long, from what I hear. They're prospecting all over the place." Bill looked interested, but said nothing, so Mr Dyer went on: "I can't build a fence all round my wheatfield. I have to hunt the pigs off as best I may."

"My brother killed one with his sheath-knife!"

"With his sheath-knife! But how could he bail him up, without a dog?"

Mr Dyer listened with amazement as Bill told the story. "He shouldn't try that again. It's too dangerous," he said. "How would you boys like to join forces with me and go out with dogs and a gun?"

"Truly – could we? Truly?"

From then on, wild pork took first place on the Phipps's dinner-table. Sometimes the boys did a few days' work for Mr Dyer, and were paid wages. With this money, Mrs Phipps bought a camp-oven. This was a big, heavy iron pot with a close-fitting lid which, standing on hot embers and covered by more hot embers, would bake the most delicious bread and scones. The little hut seemed always to breathe out the aroma of fresh-baked bread and of pork slowly roasting on the spit.

Immediately the earth began to warm and dry out, the seeds were planted and soon tiny green shoots appeared in neat rows all over the slope. "Yes, it's fertile, early land," rejoiced Mrs Phipps.

One day while pig-hunting the boys came across a sow with five little piglets. Mr Dyer took two of the piglets and the other three were put in the new chicken-run already prepared for the broody hens. Here in the evening Archie was found, happily feeding them with the family's milk which they sucked from his fingers. They were funny little reddish-coloured creatures that were soon tame enough to let Emma play with them although, being only a little creature herself, she pulled them around roughly.

As each of the first two was carried off to be made into roast sucking-pig, Archie cried and protested. As for the third one, he clung to it with such love and determination that his mother had not the heart to take it away. Soon he was following Archie everywhere, like a puppy. Archie called him Wagga.

On a warm morning in October, Mrs Phipps harvested the first spring cabbages, onions and radishes. They were carefully packed into sacks roped at both ends to be slung across the shoulders, swagger fashion; and Bill and Jack set off on the journey to market them in Lyttelton.

"Shall we spend some of the money, Mother?" Jack asked hopefully.

"Yes," she answered with her teasing smile. "I shall require needles and white thread, some linen buttons, paper for your lessons, and – saltpetre for curing bacon –"

"You shan't eat Wagga, you shan't!" cried Archie and ran outside to make sure his pet was still there. Mrs Phipps went on, "and some cup-hooks for the wall. That will do, I think. Six items."

Jack repeated the list. "Needles, thread, linen buttons, saltpetre, paper and cup-hooks, and fishing lines. Seven items."

His mother laughed with him. "Six and one make seven. You are doing well with your number lessons," she said.

The clay road was drying out with the warmer weather, although there were places where the boys had to skirt round patches of mud churned up by the hooves of horses. Above the Pinnacle they went, and around two small bays, until they mounted a hill and looked down into the wide valley beyond it. Here, where the dark trees met the rocky ridges which stretched up to the outcrop of Witch's Hill, stood a cluster of huts. This was Rapaki.

Bill and Jack had not directly encountered the Maoris. They were often seen around the Bay, gathering shellfish or fishing from their boats, which they handled expertly. They were Christians and tried to live like Europeans, but they only half succeeded. Their houses were not Maori style but built after the fashion of whalers' huts. Reeds and rushes were woven over a supplejack frame, plastered with clay and roofed with thatch, with a chimney at one end and square holes for

windows. Under the eaves there hung large eels and small
sharks drying in the sun, sending out a strong fishy smell on the
easterly breeze; and pigs ran about everywhere.

But there were two modern buildings of which the whole
village was very proud: the church and the school. Most of the
older people and all of the young ones could read and write,
which was more than could be said of many white people at
that time. It did not matter to them if their European clothes
were worn in odd ways, or if some of them still preferred a
blanket tied across the shoulders.

The boys walked silently down the hill. They felt nervous
but neither would admit it. After all, they'd lived alongside the
aborigines! But the blackfellows were slender and timid com-
pared with these burly, tattooed men who shouted "Hu! Hu!"
in deep voices as they plied their paddles over the harbour.

An old man with white hair was squatting against a sunny
wall, with his head on his knees and his blanket spread like a
tent. He did not look up until the boys were near. Then with a
sudden shout he sprang to his feet; and people appeared from
everywhere: women with babies tied in a pikau on their backs,
toddlers, boys and girls, young men, old men.

"What shall we do if they try to grab us?" whispered Jack.

"It's fatal to run away. If they touch us, we'll dodge up
the hill!"

Bill and Jack marched on. The road was too narrow to avoid
the waiting group, and a two-year-old boy leaned from a
woman's arms to catch at Jack's sandy-coloured hair. The hot
air from the pipe she was smoking blew across Jack's face, and
her eyes looked strange under her hat – a man's felt hat faded
to a dull green. Jack pushed the child away and a gabble of
voices broke out around him. Hands were everywhere; the

sack of cabbages was slipping from his shoulders; and Bill had vanished. With his throat so dry that he couldn't utter a sound, Jack ducked between the blanket-wearers and made a dash for the hill.

At first he felt sure that he was being followed by a dozen men or more; but soon the voices seemed distant and he crept behind a bush to look back. The Maoris were still clustered in the road and there was no sign of Bill.

Jack went on moving stealthily in the direction of Lyttelton, aiming for a point just above where the road crossed the next hill. Everything was very quiet. After a time he heard a low whistle from up above him, and when at last he caught a glimpse of his brother he saw with relief that Bill was still carrying his sack.

At least one of them had not been robbed! But Jack cursed his bad luck. With only half their supply of vegetables to sell, there could hardly be enough money to buy fishing-lines.

Still carefully keeping concealed from any watching eyes, the boys moved from bush to bush and hollow to hollow, coming closer until they slid together through the tussock over the brow of the hill. A thrill of triumph ran through them. They had escaped!

"Hurrah!" cried Jack and stood up – to find himself looking straight into the eyes of a Maori boy sitting alone on a bank.

He gasped and began to run. The boy ran also, shouting, and soon was ahead of them in the middle of the road. "Grab a stick, Jack, we'll stand and fight," said Bill.

Jack needed no persuading. He tore a dry branch from a fuchsia tree and stopped to size up his enemy. The Maori boy, wearing long trousers and a back-to-front sailor's jersey with one sleeve missing, stared back at them. Suddenly, like an eel he darted past and backed up the hill the way he had come. Bill and Jack watched, not moving, still grasping their sticks.

When the boy reached the skyline he lifted something up and sent it rolling towards them. Then, shouting, he flung himself into the air with both arms and legs outstretched and disappeared down the other side of the hill. The object kept on rolling.

"It's my cabbages!" cried Jack.

"They were afraid we'd tell the police," scoffed Bill. "They're awfully scared of our police."

All the same, he was not sure that this was the right explanation.

Surprise at Lyttelton

LYTTELTON was very lively. The shops all seemed busy. Men stood outside the Mitre Hotel in noisy groups, and a regular hubbub sounded from the bar. The cracking of carpenters' hammers echoed through the crisp air. Men were levelling the clay roads and ploughing gutters along the side to carry away the next fall of rain. At the wharf lay the *Zingari*, the steamship that carried mail between the North and South Islands. Some small boats were also alongside; two large ships rode at anchor; and sailing gracefully with the easterly wind behind her, a good-sized barque came into view.

The boys were passing the Steadfast Dining Rooms when one of the sash-windows was thrown up and a woman called after them:

"What have you there, boys?"

"Cabbages, spring onions and radishes," answered Bill.

"Wait! Let me see!" The woman, plump and wearing a white cap and apron, came rustling through the door. She held a knife to cut the flax cords, but Bill was not to be hurried. He untied the sacks carefully and drew out samples of his vegetables, tender green and crimson and white.

"They're *spring* cabbages – beautiful!" said the woman. "I'll give threepence each."

Jack's eyes widened. Their mother had said they might ask for twopence. But Bill saw, in the quickness of her offer, the chance of a better bargain: cabbages were scarce after all.

"Our mother said we're to go to the ships, but if they're not sold we'll bring them back," he said.

"Mind you do, then! There'll be a hot drink of tea if you want it."

They went on to the wharf. Here they displayed their produce and soon everything was sold: the cabbages for fourpence, the radishes for a penny and the spring onions for twopence a bunch. The sailors were eager for such fine fresh vegetables so early in the season; and as for the barque just coming in, she'd be out of luck.

The boats from the barque were coming ashore and the boys stayed to watch. A young woman in a plaid shawl and a pretty pink bonnet sat in the bow with her back towards them. Now she stood up and allowed the oarsman to hand her to the landing.

"Mary Ann!" cried Bill. "Look, it's Mary Ann!"

The brothers almost knocked one another into the harbour, and Mary Ann, turning quickly at the sound of her name, lost her balance and fell against the sailor's shoulder. She flushed, stammered an apology, and raising her long skirts ran up the steps. She would have liked to throw her arms around Bill's neck; but he seemed too grown up already, so she stretched out her two hands, one for each brother. The boys felt suddenly shy. They had never before seen her dressed as a fashionable young lady.

"We didn't think of you coming. And here you are, all togged out fit to kill!" said Bill.

"What was it like living in Sydney all that time?" asked Jack.

Mary Ann smiled. She was happy, yet her face was softer and sadder. "I couldn't stay in Sydney any longer – I had a big disappointment," she said.

"It wasn't Father – was it? Did he come?"

"No. It wasn't Father. A long time ago, when you'd left, I heard about him; that was all. He followed us to Sydney just after the *Armenian* sailed, and went round the shipping offices asking for Mrs Small. Mr McCracken heard about it. He didn't ask for any passage himself and he must have gone back to Berrima, we think."

"That's good news, at any rate!"

"What did you do, then?" asked Jack.

"Mrs McCracken found me a good situation. They were a doctor's family, so accomplished – every evening they were singing over the piano! I wasn't allowed in the drawing-room, of course, but I could hear from my little room and I learned all the latest songs. They had me dress their hair – that's how I learned to do mine. Do you like it this way? And on Sundays we went to church, a big church with a choir."

She stopped, and flushed again. Other people were watching and listening: did she sound too boastful? "Tell me about yourselves," she said quickly. "Mother wrote that we had a home, but that you were still working at Cashmere."

Quite forgetting Mary Ann's box, they walked slowly up the hill, exchanging their news. What the disappointment was that had hurried Mary Ann away from Sydney, she did not say. In any case they were going in and out of the shops, making the seven purchases, and Mary Ann could not help commenting on how poky the shops were after the big ones in Sydney. They went to the Steadfast Dining Rooms too, and promised the woman that she should have the next sackful of cabbages at fourpence each.

"My travelling box!" exclaimed Mary Ann, remembering. "Oh, we must go back to the wharf and fetch it!"

"Is it heavy?" asked Jack doubtfully. Up hill and down dale, all the way back to Governors Bay, and through Rapaki, they would have to carry that box!

"Oh yes – I've bought a heap of new things," she said brightly, "but I'll help with it myself, of course."

But they had a stroke of luck. Mr Parsons was at the wharf, setting up the sail on his boat, for the breeze was still blowing up the harbour; and the boys helped him stack his goods to make room for them all. "I'm delighted to hear you have come, Miss Phipps," he said in his gentlemanly way. "Your mother will be glad of your help, I'm sure. She spends all day in the garden."

Mary Ann thanked him for his courtesy, and he could not have guessed how startled she was to be addressed, without hesitation, as Miss *Phipps*.

Nothing was seen of Rapaki as they sailed past, except curls of smoke rising above the trees and a number of half-naked figures gathering pauas by the headland.

The little cob hut, with her mother and all her family there, was cosy and comforting to Mary Ann. True, it was a squeeze

to get everybody in; Bill and Jack were still sleeping on the
floor of the little bedroom at nights, and Emma would have
to top-and-tail with her mother to give Mary Ann, who was
taller than anyone except Bill, a bunk to sleep in. But how
pretty it all looked as Emma and Jimmy took her to the
spring; through the bush with its kowhai already golden and
along the beach scattered with shells, white and gold and
mauve, and the sea gleaming in the evening light! That night
there was rejoicing because the garden had brought its first
profits, and the last of the family had come to the new home.
No piano was needed as Mrs Phipps sang the old familiar
ballads in the firelight, and Mary Ann sang the new ones she
had learned in Sydney, until Emma fell asleep across her sister's
knees and Jim could fight back his drowsiness no longer.

In the midst of it came a knock on the door and a deep voice
calling in words that nobody could understand.

Maoris!

Jack made a leap for the bedroom as Mrs Phipps lifted the
door-latch. How could she do it so calmly! Bill flattened
himself against the wall where he could not be seen. But only
one face appeared, a tattooed face over neat European coat
and trousers.

"I come to speak of the tamariki," said the stranger.

"Tamariki?" repeated Mrs Phipps. She thought at first that
he meant animals, but he pointed to the sleeping Emma.

"Tamariki – children. The tall children. Boys."

"You have lost your boys?"

"No. I speak of the boys from this house. They come by
Rapaki in the morning and they do not return. We watch,
and we grow afraid, for you."

In all the excitement of the home-coming, Mrs Phipps had

been told nothing about Rapaki except a few words from Jack about having been chased; boastful words about having regained his lost sack. But the speed with which the boys had disappeared from view was enough, and she said mischievously:

"They are not here just now, but they are not lost. Would you like me to send them to you tomorrow?"

She caught a glimpse of Bill's horrified stare as the Maori answered calmly:

"Not tomorrow. Some time we will see them. I come only so that, if they are lost, we may find them for you; for the land is an open book to us."

"Thank you," said Mrs Phipps with a grave courtesy that matched her visitor's. "I'm very much obliged, and I will speak to the boys."

"Kia ora," said the Maori in courteous farewell. Mrs Phipps waited until he had passed from the beam of firelight which stretched from the doorway, then latched the door and sank back into her packing-case chair, helpless with gay laughter. Shame-faced, Bill and Jack crept back to the hearth.

"They chased you!" she said. "They took your sack and you made them give it back! Ah! It was only curiosity – and if you'd had *your* share of it, you wouldn't have made such fools of yourselves!"

12

Wagga

MARY ANN said nothing more to her brothers about the disappointment that had hurried her home from Sydney; but from the talk that went on between her and Mrs Phipps, it plainly had something to do with a young man. He had gone away, back to England; and she, not able to face the thought of never seeing her own family again, had let him go without her.

"I knew you would need me, Mother," she said, "and all the fine ladies of Sydney aren't worth as much as you."

It was true that Mary Ann was needed; for Mrs Phipps spent all the daylight hours working in the garden, and could now leave all the housework and cooking to her daughter. But the house was far too small. Bill, Jack and Archie had to set to work building a new room on to the end of the cob hut.

The cost was small, but it took hours and hours of work. First they had to cut strong, straight poles of kowhai and drive them into the ground for uprights. To this frame they fixed laths made of thin sticks of manuka, rather like concrete boxing; and into the space between they pressed the cob, which was clay and chopped tussock mixed with water like a mud pie. When it dried out, hard as brick, the laths were taken away and the wall smoothed and white-washed. The roof was thatched with tussock and the room fitted with a door opening on to the outside path, a glazed calico window of its own, and four new bunks. The tiny original bedroom was left clear for Mrs Phipps, Mary Ann and Emma.

During the building, Wagga blundered happily about the place knocking over tubs of water and clay with the greatest freedom. This was a great nuisance; for all the water had to be carried from the spring in wooden buckets balanced two at a time on a shoulder-yoke. Mary Ann thought a pet piglet was quite ridiculous and drove him away from the kitchen door; but the others forgave him, and Archie succeeded in keeping him off the garden.

When the boys were not building they were carrying vegetables to Lyttelton. Before long Mrs Phipps went too, with a basket of the first strawberries on her arm. At Rapaki the Maoris came out to admire the kete (kit) which did not hang loosely like their own, but displayed the berries prettily arranged in a nest of their own leaves. Mrs Phipps had fashioned the kete with a hoop and a handle of supplejack and with green flax interlaced between.

The Phipps's produce was earning fame. Buyers learned to

watch for it, and ships' cooks would order supplies for the next time they came into port. But there was much waste of time and labour in carrying everything on human backs and arms, and so Mrs Phipps would buy nothing that was not absolutely needed, but put aside something out of every sale towards buying a boat. Knowing that this boat was Jack's great dream, she let him hide away the money in a secret place.

As the green crops were harvested she planted potatoes, carrots and parsnips, which would grow through the dry summer. Already there were gooseberries and currants, red and black. All of these were picked for sale and only the under-sized or squashy ones used for the children. Mrs Phipps did not, like most parents in those days, use the stick freely to discipline her family, for she had seen too much of harsh beatings. All the same, a supplejack was kept handy for anyone seen taking the fruit.

There was hardly any time for lessons: only on wet days. There was no time for games either, but the boys could cool off by swimming in the Bay, and with the new lines they went fishing at the Pinnacle. Jack spent odd moments at the fireside in whittling small boats. He inserted masts and bowsprits, joined on long ropes of plaited flax, and had Mary Ann make sails out of scraps of old linen. Jim, whose main job was looking after Emma, spent hours with her on the beach sailing these boats and rescuing the rag doll, Bibi, who proved to be a most unsteady sailor and was now looking like a washed-up piece of fish.

As summer drew on, Wagga changed from a piglet into a young pig. His reddish coat began to turn iron-grey, and he was no longer content with the scraps that Archie fed to him.

He wanted to root for himself; and although Archie tried to keep him to the fern, Wagga dodged back and made a meal of new potatoes. On the very same day he pulled down and trampled some clean clothes which Mary Ann had spread over the bushes to dry. This was a serious crime, for washing was hard work with only buckets to wash in.

Mrs Phipps backed up Mary Ann's complaint. "Archie, a piglet is a pet, but a full-grown pig is not. You must let him go!"

"He isn't *very* big yet," pleaded Archie, although he was dismayed himself at the speed with which Wagga had grown. At least his mother hadn't said, "You must let him be eaten." So Archie hardened his heart and sent Wagga away – but Wagga came back, every time.

After the third try, Mrs Phipps said:

"You must take him right to the top of the Saddle above Mr Dyer's, and let him go from there. He'll soon find other pigs to be friends with, and then he won't fret for you."

Archie plodded unwillingly up the hill. It was lunch-time when he came out of the bush and there, sitting on a sunny bank, were four men with a billy steaming over a fire. They had been levelling off the new road from Cashmere. The men thought it very funny to see a boy followed by what looked at first like a dog, but gave out most un-dog-like grunts and snuffles.

"Taking him to market, sonny?" asked one with a bushy black beard.

"No," said Archie. "This is Wagga. He's my pet but he's grown too big, so I've got to let him go bush."

"Now here's a case!" said the man, and the other three all laughed uproariously while Archie, to whom it was not at all funny, stood quite still, not knowing whether to go or to stay. Then another man said seriously:

"What will happen to him when he goes bush?"

"He'll find a lady pig – a sow – and get married."

The men thought this sensible explanation was funny, too.

"Supposing he won't settle down to bush life with his sow?"

"He wouldn't stay when we sent him away at home," said Archie, "but up here he won't be able to find us, so he'll get used to it."

"Chase him into the bush and see," said a third man, reaching mysteriously behind his lunch-bag.

Archie's quick eyes saw the movement, and something froze inside him. The man had a gun! Of course, they must keep it handy in case wild pigs came around when they were working – but Wagga wasn't a wild pig; of this, there must be no mistake. "I'm going to take him, not chase him," said Archie.

He went a long way into the bush, meaning to find a small bluff where Wagga could be dropped over without harm but could not scramble up again. A good place was not hard to find and soon Archie was alone, with Wagga's surprised grunts growing fainter and his own face hard set, because he was too old to cry.

When he came out the men were putting away their billy and pannikins, and taking up their tools. Archie nodded and marched silently past. Then he heard a call:

"You think you lost him, sonny?"

Archie swung round. There stood Wagga exactly where he had himself come from the bush. If Wagga had run back, or run to him! But he'd learned to be friendly to all humans.

He went up to the black-bearded man and stood happily waiting for some titbit or mark of interest.

"Stand back, Hal!" said the man with the gun.

It was all done in a minute. The shooter was so near that he could not possibly miss. Archie did not even wait to see his pet fall. He ran wildly down the hill, into the cool dark of the bush, feeling the tears rush from his eyes in spite of himself. Even here, the sound of the shot seemed to echo without end. When he came within sight of his own cottage he could not bear the sight of that, either, with no Wagga any more. He wheeled off into the trees and slid down a bank into a private nook, with his feet in the cold water of the Bay; there to stay hidden until it was almost dark and hunger grew stronger than his sorrow.

"Wherever have you been? There's no wood chopped, and we called and called," said Mary Ann sharply.

But after dinner Mrs Phipps sat patiently alone with Archie in the new room until the story was at last confided.

"They take all my pets away," he whispered.

"We shall have to find a pet that's useful too, Archie, even when it grows up."

"I don't want an old goat," he said, for she had often spoken of buying milking-goats. "They're no fun."

"What if it should be a puppy?"

"Puppies aren't useful," said Archie, determined at that moment not to love anything but Wagga.

"They *can* be, and you know it, Archie. Of course they take a deal of keeping in meat, and you would have to train it to work."

"A big one – like Mr Dyer's?"

"Yes, if you choose it, Archie."

When he was at last in bed – his brothers, for once, fast asleep before him – he tossed about all night, bothered by dreams in which Wagga became a dog, and Mr Dyer's dog became Wagga, and men with guns were strangely put to flight and lost over bluffs in the bush. In the morning he began thinking, but not too urgently or hopefully, about puppies.

13

Hard-working Summer

THE secret hoard of money grew and grew; but just when Jack was almost certain that the boat would be bought for Christmas, the savings came to a stop. The green vegetables were nearly all harvested and sold, when a scorching nor'west gale swept over the Saddle to flatten most of the rest of the garden. The green peas dried up; and there were only the beans to sell until the root crops were ready.

The Phipps family had a short lull in their busy days to make Christmas presents for one another. They whittled spinning-tops out of wood, stripped the flax and plaited whips, and made quaint ornaments with shells and pebbles. Mary Ann cut up old black stockings to make a golliwog for Emma. It was hard work sewing up the black stuff, when Emma was asleep, by the dim light of the slush-lamp; if only she had Mrs McCracken's sewing-machine now! But Emma's delight on Christmas morning repaid her for everything. The golliwog's round red smile was matched by her own, and she went round all morning singing "Boola boy, Boola boy..."

As for Christmas dinner, a young rooster made the main dish and there was a marvellous plum duff, a "spotty Dick", well studded with currants.

For the first time they all went to Christmas service in the cob hut a mile-and-a-half farther up the Bay, just below the "church acre" where the people planned to build a real church very soon. Green ferns decorated the makeshift altar and a violin played for the carols. Afterwards the families lingered in the warm sunshine and talked, for church was the only social occasion they ever had; and Mrs Phipps met the settlers she had been far too busy to get to know – the Vigers, the Beecheys, the Hodgsons, the Dobbses and the Calverts.

With the New Year, Bill and Jack were in great demand as labourers for the harvest. Several farmers were growing wheat and barley, which must be cut and stacked by hand. The boys brought home their wages, thinking they would go into the hoard for buying the boat; but this time Mrs Phipps said firmly, "No!"

"It's needed for something more important – even than the boat, Jack."

"Mother – it can't be!"

"We sweated up there all day in the sun –" grumbled Bill.

"And we can't carry *potatoes* to Lyttelton! We *must* have a boat!"

"What could be more important?"

"Your schooling, boys," she said.

"Schooling!" Bill said scornfully. "I can read good enough – and besides I work with my hands. They reckon I work good."

"A bit of brain to guide your hands won't be wasted, Bill. At least you'll master enough figuring not to be taken down; and you can hold your heads up anywhere."

"But we're too big for school," argued Jack. "We're doing man's work, we are!"

Mary Ann seized her turn.

"If we could change places I know what I'd do!" she cried. "I'd give my best bonnet for the chance you've got. I've seen myself – serving tea to young ladies who could talk with gentlemen and not give themselves away every time they opened their mouths. *He* wanted me to go to England – and what if I'd gone, and couldn't talk to his people? I was too scared. I hate being ignorant, I hate it!"

She stamped her foot, angry with the whole world, and the boys did not dare say another word in protest.

School began as soon as the harvest was over. Mr and Mrs Parsons had a little schoolroom, twelve feet by twelve, in their own small house. Here sat a dozen children at all stages of learning; some painfully drawing their letters on their slates, big boys though they were; others studying mathematics, history, Latin and Greek. They walked or rode from miles away, ten boys and two girls, bringing their copybooks and pencils, and threepence a day for the teacher.

Mrs Phipps sold some eggs and young roosters and bought two goats, which Archie learned to milk. Besides saving money, Mrs Phipps thought this would be better than going to Mr Dyer for milk, since in January he had been married. The wedding was a simple affair. He had ridden off to Christchurch at seven in the morning, leaving Joe Munnings, the young man who worked for him, to straighten up the house, groom the bullocks and take the sledge down to the road. In the evening the bride came to her new home riding in the bullock-sledge as gaily as if it had been a carriage.

Mr Dyer worked with fresh enthusiasm to improve his farm. Impatient with the endless work of clearing the fern, he chose a gentle morning in March to set a match to it. The nor'east breeze carried the fire upwards; he expected it to be stopped by the rocky ledges near the ridge. But Mrs Phipps, seeing the glow high on the hills after darkness had fallen that day, was uneasy. She had seen bush-fires in Australia, and thought of them with awe and fear; besides, she knew how quickly the Canterbury winds could change.

During the night, the nor'easter did indeed swing round to the nor'west and Mr Dyer awoke in the morning to a strong smell of smoke.

He hurried to a knob near by and saw that the fire was burning downhill through fresh fern, across the property of his nearest neighbour, Mr Beechey. Between the fire and the Bay were a number of houses and also the timber stacked in readiness for building the church. Still, it did not appear dangerous and the green patches of tutu should hold it back. He found Joe Munnings quietly milking the cows, and went in to breakfast, saying nothing to alarm his wife.

When he came to have a second look, he met Bill and Jack Phipps coming up carrying sacks, axes and a slasher.

"Mother says you'll be needing us," said Bill bluntly.

"But you can't see the fire from *your* place?"

"We can see the smoke and the direction of the wind – that's enough!"

Mr Dyer went into action at once.

"I'll take my horse and go out and warn everyone. We'll meet – let me see – at the church acre. That's the way it's going. Bill, would you find Joe Munnings, and tell Mrs Dyer I've gone? Only please take care not to alarm her!"

As he galloped down the hill, Mr Dyer saw Archie Phipps coming up alone. He looked very small, he was only ten years old, after all, and Mr Dyer wondered that his mother should let him come. But he could not stop to talk.

The nor'wester was now blowing in strong gusts. With every burst of wind the fire blazed and widened. The settlers did not need to be roused and were out already when Mr Dyer appeared. There was no hope of stopping it in the fern; and so it was decided to cut back the tutu and scrub in a deep line above the houses. This meant working in the thick of the smoke, where each man could see only the next in the line, and with the stifling nor'wester in their faces.

Soon the women were in action too. Billies of cool water and hot tea, baskets of bread and scones were carried the length of the line. When sparks blew across the unfinished firebreak, the wives took up sacks to beat them out.

Mary Ann brought Jim and Emma with her to Mrs Dobbs's house, and helped with the baking, for she was quicker at this than anyone else. Jim found himself minding the Dobbs's baby as well as Emma – a sad task for a boy whose brothers were fire-fighting. Mrs Phipps took a tea-billy up the hill herself. She knew that Archie had gone, without her permission, to join his brothers; but she was not out to bring him home. If he were in the road, the men would send him away. Still, as she handed out pannikins of tea she asked quietly if anyone had seen Archie; and she was about to go down without an answer when she heard a hoarse voice calling her.

"Mother! Mother..."

Bill was coming out of the smoke with Archie in his arms. He was stumbling, for his eyes were wet and blurred, and Archie lay quite limp, half-suffocated.

Her quick eyes summed everything up at once.

"Bill – are *you* all right?"

"It's only the smoke," he said, coughing.

"And were you with Jack?"

"Yes, he's still there."

"You must stay with him; keep together, do you hear? I'll take care of Archie. I've got a broad enough back."

She was quite determined. As soon as Bill could muster enough strength to lift his brother, she took Archie's weight across her shoulders and grasped his wrists and ankles.

"Mother, let me come," pleaded Bill.

"No. You must stay with Jack – when you come, come together," she commanded.

With slow, careful steps she descended the hill. She could not stop to rest, because there was no one to lift Archie up again if she did. All the while she gave a silent prayer that Archie would come round safely – and with it, a joy and pride came to her, that her children had all grown sturdy in this hard, clean life.

Nobody saw her coming. She tapped her hardest on Mrs Dobbs's door with the toe of her boot. Footsteps came quickly, the door opened and Mrs Phipps lost her balance and fell through on to the bare board floor.

"Mother!" cried Mary Ann in a fright.

Somewhere beyond her, Emma sobbed: "Mumma, Mumma!"

"Archie," said Mrs Phipps, and fainted.

Even in the house, smoke was everywhere except in the bedroom, where Mrs Dobbs had plugged every crack to keep the air clear for her sleeping baby. Mary Ann and Mrs Dobbs laid Mrs Phipps on the bed and Archie on the floor, banging the door shut in the frightened faces of Jim and Emma, who began to bawl loudly. This was no time for explaining anything. It was puzzle enough to know where to begin; but Mary Ann knew that whenever there was a doubt, her mother's word was law; and her mother had said *Archie*.

"She'll come round by herself," she said firmly. "It's Archie who's suffocated."

The two women turned him on his back and gently moved his arms and shoulders to work some air into his lungs. The baby woke and began to whimper. Mrs Phipps stirred at this sound and hung her head over the side of the bed, sighing. The two children outside continued to bawl, and there was hardly room to move.

"Oh," gasped Mrs Dobbs, "if only we had some real fresh air!"

She swayed. Mary Ann thought with terror: am I to have them *all* on my hands? Forgetting everything else she pulled out the cloth that plugged the window-sill and threw up the sash.

Cool, sweet air flowed in from beyond the head of the Bay.

"The wind's changed!" cried Mary Ann. "Mrs Dobbs, it's gone to sou'west! Mother, Mother, it's changed!"

Mrs Dobbs leaned out and breathed deeply. "Yes, it's sou'west – praised be the Lord!"

Archie began to cough. Mrs Dobbs lifted her baby to comfort him and Mary Ann opened the door to her terrified brother and sister. Emma scrambled up on to the bed and cuddled close to her half-conscious mother; and the cold wind blew deliciously over them.

Up on the hill the men saw the smoke curling away to reveal one blackened face after another. They could hardly believe their good fortune. The fire, no longer fierce, began to burn back in a slanting line to where it had first been lit. If the sou'wester held, it would certainly burn itself out.

Bill and Jack sat down to rest their heads on their knees. It took a long spell before they could think of a fresh worry.

"Bill," said Jack, stretching up, "what if it burns down to our place?"

"How could it? It's burning uphill."

"But if the wind came down again?"

"We'd soon know."

"What's happened to Archie?"

"He's at my place, with your mother, quite safe," said a voice, and Jack looked up to see Mrs Dobbs holding out a pannikin of water. He thanked her and drank gratefully, and stood up.

"I'm off home. I want to see it's all right," he said.

Although common sense told him that the fire could not possibly have touched the house, Jack couldn't rest until he had made sure. Bill went with him, but as they reached a high point and saw for themselves that the fire was beyond danger, he exclaimed:

"I don't suppose I'll be around here much longer."

"What d'you mean?" asked Jack.

"What is there for me here? One day I'm a schoolboy, next

day I'm a hired labourer. Something happens like this fire and I'm as good as the next man, and better than most. I could make my way anywhere."

"Where would you go, Bill?" Jack wasn't sure whether to admire his brother's boldness or to jibe at his boasting.

"I'm not sure yet," said Bill seriously. "It might be Nelson."

A vague connection stirred in Jack's mind.

"Nelson? Did they find gold in Nelson?"

"Somewhere thereabouts. I'd go if there was a real *big* strike. Whatever anyone said."

A weird, high-pitched cry sounded suddenly from the direction of the cottage. Goldfields forgotten, Jack began to run – the haunting vision of his own home going up in flames returning.

But the clearing, the garden, the white walls were exactly as they had been left. Only the two goats strained at their tethers and bleated in protest because it was time for their milking.

14

Through the Storm

ALTHOUGH it was only autumn, there came a burst of winter
with a "southerly buster" which raged for six days. No one
could go to school, for the dry gullies became rivers, and the
tracks were impassable with mud. The roar of the waves and
the gale in the trees filled day and night with noise.

Snug and warm with a good stack of firewood and a huge
pan of broth always simmering, the Phipps family had spent
the third day indoors with their needlework and their lessons.
Even Emma borrowed a slate and made letters and drawings
which looked like scribbles to everyone else, but were full of
meanings for herself. When daylight gave out, books had to be
put away. After the meal, the family gathered around the fire.

"A story now, Mumma!" said Jim.

"Story," sang Emma, "story, story!"

Bill and Jack took out the draught-board and settled down to play, while Mary Ann sat quietly knitting. Mrs Phipps began with Emma's favourite – the Old Woman and her Pig.

They had reached the point where for the seventh time the piggy wouldn't jump over the stile, when Archie interrupted from his place by the door.

"Somebody's knocking."

"Hark, everyone!"

There was a hush, but nothing was heard except the storm and the crackling of the fire. "Who would find their way down here on a night like this?" said Mrs Phipps.

"Go on with the story," begged Jim.

"So the old woman went a little farther and she found a butcher –'

Archie turned his head sharply, stretched over and lifted the latch. The door swung open with the force of the wind behind it.

A young Maori woman stood there, wrapped in a cloak of coarse flax, with a little girl in front of her. The woman had a pikau on her back, but whether there was a baby in it nobody could tell. They were like two sodden statues.

"Why, come inside!" cried Mrs Phipps. "You can't stand there in this weather. Mary Ann, put the kettle on!"

The woman nodded gravely and pushed the girl before her into the room. Behind them now appeared a very old woman with a tattooed chin and wrinkled cheeks. Water poured from them and over their bare muddy feet. The tiny room was crammed with people.

"Back, children, and let them come to the fire! Never

mind the wet – we must get some warmth into you," said Mrs Phipps.

The children pressed back to the wall, and Mary Ann pushed the kettle and the soup pan over the blaze, and hurried to the bedroom. The old woman began to speak rapidly in Maori. Mrs Phipps took her hands and drew her to the hearth; the hands were numb and stiff. Shyly the little girl came to the warmth.

"Boys!" commanded Mrs Phipps. "All to bed! There's work to be done here. Archie, take Emma, please."

"Story! I want the story!"

"No, Emma."

"I'll tell you the story in your bed," whispered Archie as he took her in his arms. At the bedroom entrance they had to dodge Mary Ann who was almost hidden behind an armful of blankets.

The young mother lifted down the pikau. Yes, there was a baby, a sad little thing that barely moved and had not enough strength to cry.

"Mumma," whispered Jim, "is the baby dead?"

"No, but it's very ill, I think. You must go to bed; we'll be very busy making it better."

The boys had to run around the house to their own bedroom entrance, and a gust from the door sent a shiver through the room. Already Mary Ann had begun work on the girl, stripping off her clothes and rubbing her dry. The old woman, with a few quiet words, loosened her own cloak and let the heat from the fire draw the steam away; she moved her arms gently and rhythmically to restore the circulation. The young mother sat without moving, quite exhausted.

"Let me take the baby," said Mrs Phipps kindly. "You must get yourself dry."

"He's very sick," said the mother.

The baby's hands and feet were icy but his forehead burned in a hot flush under the brown skin. Mrs Phipps held him to the fire, rubbing him gently, as she had often done with a weakling calf. By this time the little girl had a warm blanket wrapped round her naked body and was sipping her bowl of hot broth. Mary Ann set the teapot to brew and helped the young mother to change. Only when she had taken her cup of strong, sweet tea did she have strength enough to speak.

"My husband is away at Akaroa," said the mother at last. "The water washes the houses at Rapaki – our house, many others, full of water. We come here."

"You did right to come," Mrs Phipps assured her. "I have been through Rapaki, but I do not know your names."

"This is Mrs Tau, my husband's grandmother." The old woman looked up and nodded at the mention of her own name.

"You are Mrs Tau, too?"

"I am Mrs Tau; I am Miria. The girl, Eita – Esther. The boy, Wiremu – very sick."

"Wiremu? That's William, isn't it? We also have a William! You have milk for the baby, have you?"

"He will not drink. He will die."

Her voice was without hope, and so was the tone of the Maori words that came rapidly from Mrs Tau. Those old eyes had seen many sorrows. Before the white settlement, the war-parties of the great chief Te Rauparaha had come from the north and killed many of their kinsmen. There had even been a long feud within their own Ngai-Tahu tribe. Measles and influenza, brought by the pakeha, had taken many Maori lives. Was it likely that this little one could be saved?

Miria repeated a little of this in English, but Mrs Phipps would have no such talk.

"Where there's life, there's hope. You have milk?"

"Yes, I have milk."

"Then I shall make him wake now, and cry, and when he cries you must force him to swallow. Perhaps he will only swallow a drop. Never mind that: you must *make* him."

She slapped the baby hard until his lips parted in a loud wail, then pressed him into Miria's arms. Miria looked quite bewildered; but a gleam came into Mrs Tau's eyes and she began to talk, nodding quickly in approval. Every time little Wiremu's mouth could be made to open, he could be given a few drops.

Eita slid slowly on to the hearth, fast asleep. Mary Ann carried her into the bedroom and laid her in her own bunk. Then she made toast to go with the broth for Mrs Tau, after which the old woman settled herself in the corner and brought out a pipe and tobacco, drying it carefully before the fire. Soon the strong smell of tobacco-smoke drifted through the house. Horrified, Mary Ann glanced at her mother; but Mrs Phipps paid no attention.

When the baby had drunk a little and could be allowed to rest, Miria took food for herself. "We others shall not be in bed tonight," whispered Mrs Phipps. "You must go, Mary Ann."

"The girl is in my bunk."

"Then you must take mine."

Mary Ann knew this was no time for argument – although there were no blankets left, and she must sleep in her clothes with her shawls drawn over her.

All night the fire was kept alight and Miria fed with broth, bread and tea. Every hour the baby was awakened and made to swallow; but his cries did not wake the sleepers, not even his great-grandmother propped in the corner. Only when her own children were astir in the morning did Mrs Phipps think it time to send Miria and little Wiremu to lie down. As for herself, the day's work was beginning as usual.

The storm continued for three more days. Flour ran low, and no stores could be brought in, but there were always potatoes to fill the pot. "Ah," said Miria, "at Rapaki we have dried shark. When we go home, we will send you the dried shark!"

She was no longer weary and hopeless, for baby Wiremu was almost well. The fever had left him, and his face had puckered that morning into a true baby smile, given to an adoring Emma! Eita chattered and played, and Miria herself was like a big girl, laughing and singing, and delighted that the boys had a draught-board. At Rapaki, all the Maoris loved to play draughts! And could they do stick-games? After Jack had whittled enough sticks from the woodpile they sat on the floor in a circle while Miria sang, and taught them how to clap the sticks together and toss them from one to another in all sorts of ways. How she laughed when the sticks slipped from their hands and clattered down! And then Eita discovered Emma's doll Bibi, neglected since Boola had come at Christmas-time, and spent hours wrapping her in pieces of rag. Mrs Phipps, who loved to sing at her work, was startled to hear a soft and perfect harmony joining the familiar Old Country melodies. Sometimes there was even a triple harmony when Mrs Tau came in with her deep voice; but mostly the old woman merely sat and smoked.

It was like camping, with the house so full that people were apologizing all day for pushing past or falling over one another. But at the first beam of sunshine, every child dashed outside and danced madly on the muddy earth, except little Wiremu who slept in peaceful contentment.

When the tracks had dried out and the creeks had fallen, the Tau family went away.

"We will come again!" cried Miria. "We send you the dried shark!"

15

The Boat

THE gift of dried shark was brought the following Sunday afternoon by two Maori boys in a canoe. Mrs Phipps was called down to the beach to receive it. She thanked the bringers very nicely, in spite of her private doubts as to whether her family would enjoy the shark.

But there was no doubt about the canoe. It was the first time any of them had taken a close look at one, and before long it had shot out of sight beyond the Pinnacle, with Jack trying his hand at the paddle. At Rapaki Bay he practised over and over, up and down, to the encouraging shouts and laughing comments of the Maoris on the beach – Miria and Eita among them. When at last he beached the canoe, a very dignified rangatira, Mr Mahurangi, came forward.

"Your hand is well fashioned for the paddle," he said.

"It's a capital canoe, sir," said Jack, returning the compliment.

"You have need of a boat. I see you passing with many burdens."

"Yes, we're saving money to buy one. We've got seven pounds and we'll need ten. There's the potatoes still to dig – but we don't know. Some of the money'll be needed for the winter."

Mr Mahurangi pondered this problem. Then he said:

"There are pakehas who cannot paddle even a light canoe. Such a one would sell a good boat at a small price. Tell your mother to be ready with her offer."

Jack ran home and eagerly passed on the message. He took these mysterious words to be a promise, but his mother was not at all sure. When Bill suggested Jack should go back and ask Mr Mahurangi what he meant, she forbade him firmly. "They have their own kind of pride," she said. "If it's a promise, it will be fulfilled in good time; and if it's not, we'll be none the worse off."

The next day they began digging the potatoes. It was a fine crop, but as the pile grew, so did the problem of getting it all to Lyttelton. Mrs Phipps spoke of engaging one of the Lyttelton watermen to bring a good-sized boat with a punt in tow; but this would mean taking money from the savings to pay for someone else's boat. The more Jack thought about this, the less he liked it, and he made up his mind that next Sunday he would ignore his mother's orders and seek out Mr Mahurangi.

Then this little plan was spoiled because on that Sunday

he had to go looking for Jim and Emma, who had not come in for midday dinner.

They were not on the beach where they had been playing. They could not have gone far along the shore, because it was high tide right up to the banks, and the trees where they often made houses or swung on the supplejacks were deserted. It was very strange. Mrs Phipps set everyone to looking in the most unlikely places.

In mid-afternoon, the anxious mother came back to find the lost children sitting in the sun by the door.

"We're hungry," announced Jim.

"Where have you been?" she scolded. "Dinner was long ago! You go without."

"We've been in the boat," said Jim happily, as if it were well worth missing a meal.

"In the boat!" echoed Emma.

"What boat?" demanded Mrs Phipps.

"He said it was *our* boat and you're to see if you like it."

"Who is *he*, Jim?"

Jim only grinned, jumped up and darted down the track with Emma running after him.

On the bank sat Mr Mahurangi with a boy called Taroa. They were contentedly watching the water on which floated a new-looking double-ended dinghy. Mr Mahurangi rose when he saw Mrs Phipps following the children, and introduced himself politely.

"You will have heard my message from your son, Mrs Phipps. Here is a boat waiting for your offer."

So it *was* a promise! Mrs Phipps didn't know what to say.

"You did not believe it would come so soon?" said Mr Mahurangi.

She did not like to say that she had not believed at all, so she said: "Why, Mr Mahurangi, it's the very boat we want! But I'm a gardening woman and I don't know what price I should offer."

"The owner paid ten pounds for it, but it is not worth ten pounds to him because he can only row it in circles and run it into the bank. Moreover, it has no sail. I think he would be pleased to receive seven pounds."

"That's exactly the money I have saved!" said Mrs Phipps.

"I have promised to bring back either the money or the boat. Now I will leave the boat. Jack has tried his skill with the paddles, but this boat has oars. Taroa will show him how to row it."

"Jack? But Bill is older!"

"It is Jack who has love for the sea."

He was quite right. Jack, though only thirteen, was the one to be entrusted with the boat.

"I shall go and fetch the money," said Mrs Phipps.

While this wonderful deal was being arranged, Jack was knocking on doors farther up the Bay to ask if anyone had seen Emma or Jim. When everyone had said no, he made for home, and found his mother at the cottage.

"They're found, I suppose!" he said, very annoyed.

"Yes, they came home."

"By themselves? I hope they got a good hiding for running away!"

"They didn't exactly run away."

"They spoiled my day, the little tikes!" shouted Jack.

"D'you think your day is spoiled, Jack?" said his mother with a gentle smile. "Go down to the beach."

He saw the mischievous twinkle in her eye and his anger

began to go down. Where was everyone else, anyway? And what was at the beach?

Jack ran out and down the path, and there were Archie and Jim wading through the water. But Taroa from Rapaki was there too and he pushed them back, calling out:

"Not your turn, not your turn! Look, Jack! This your boat!"

16

A Visitor Received

BEFORE the potatoes could be loaded on to the boat, which was romantically named the *Garden Queen*, the boys had to build a landing-stage. They cut away the bank to make a level platform just above high tide mark, and extended it with logs. A light sledge could be hauled by ropes on a sloping track leading down to the landing. Then it took several journeys and much hard rowing to land the whole crop at Lyttelton, but once that was done, they could use the boat to go fishing. The catch was much better well out on the harbour, and sometimes they went beyond Quail Island for cockles and oysters.

Buying the sail would have to wait for the spring. The

potato money was needed for more seeds and fruit trees, grain for the hens, the first cow – and a puppy for Archie. The collie was to be trained; but Archie had dreams of teaching him to jump and do tricks as well, so he called him Wallaby, or Wally for short.

The future looked promising for the second year at the Bay. Yet, although Mrs Phipps never spoke of it, she knew well that they lived under a double danger. It was still possible that Stephen Small might trace them and demand the right to rule his family. He would have the law on his side, for they were runaways after all.

Also they were living on land from which they could be turned off at any time. Sooner or later they must buy it, or pay rent for it. But Mrs Phipps kept well away from Cashmere. She had heard that Mr Cracroft Wilson was busy with public affairs, and her few acres were nothing to the thousands on his expanding sheep-runs. Let him come in his own good time and she would have all the more to show him.

Summer brought flowers into bloom until the cottage was almost hidden. Archways and pyramids of supplejack were built to carry the honeysuckle, jasmine, sweet peas and climbing roses. A wide border began with mignonette and mounted through tall yellow daisies and blue larkspurs to hollyhocks touching the thatched roof. There was profit as well as beauty in these flowers, which were in demand for the Lyttelton hotels.

And then those once-neglected young trees produced their very first cherries. Jim carefully counted them.

"Thirty-seven," he said. "I *think* it makes thirty-seven. It might be thirty-eight. Will they be worth a lot of money, Mother?"

"If you can work out how many we would each have, Jim," she said smiling, "we shan't sell them. We could have a little party."

When she counted them herself, it came to thirty-nine, because Jim could not see the top ones. To divide thirty-nine by seven was beyond Jim's powers, but he was not to be beaten. He collected thirty-nine shells from the beach and arranged them in seven heaps. There were five shells in each heap but he could not think what to do with the four that were over.

"I think we will give an extra cherry to the four youngest," said Mrs Phipps.

"Jack's not a nipper – we should toss for it," protested Bill. But before Jack could answer back, Bill's mouth opened and his face froze; he swung round and fled down the track to the beach. Looking to see what his brother had seen, Jack gave a yell and followed.

"It's the Nabob!" he shouted as he ran.

They were not really afraid, but they wanted no reminders of those wretched weeks at Cashmere. Archie, Jim and Emma would not have moved for anything: they almost forgot the cherries in their admiration for the gentleman with the silver-mounted riding-crop sitting with such dignity on his beautiful horse.

Mrs Phipps looked down at her muddy gardening boots and decided not to worry.

"Welcome to your property, sir," she said. "You must do me the honour to step inside and see the cottage. Mary Ann! Put the kettle on and we'll have a cup of tea."

Mr Cracroft Wilson was surprised to hear Mary Ann's name called, for he remembered nothing about a daughter left behind in Sydney. He was even more surprised to find himself stepping beneath an archway of roses into a room so sweet-smelling and colourful that he did not even notice that the furniture was made of bush logs, packing-cases, flax and sacking.

"I commend your industry, Mrs Phipps," he said, watching Mary Ann's capable hands, "though I don't know what you are – tenant or squatter."

"You could call me a caretaker, or a guardian, or a manager, as you wish."

"A caretaker would hand in reports. I have had no direct word in all the months you have been here."

"I've been writing the report every day. You can read it for yourself – in the house and the garden."

He stared at her, puzzled, so she went on:

"We came to a hut with two small rooms full of rats and litter and with leaking thatch; and a potato patch the size of a pocket-handkerchief half ruined by the wild pigs. You see a cottage enlarged and in perfect order, a garden, an orchard, a fowl-run and grazing for a cow. All this without a penny of your money or an hour of your supervision. You will ap-preciate this, sir, being renowned for your own capability in managing your estates."

The Nabob was quite baffled by this little speech. Was she being properly respectful, or was she laughing at him? He was both master and guest in the cottage and he had to act accordingly. He nodded gravely.

"Your report is satisfactory," he said, as he took the cup from Mary Ann and drank without noticing that the tea had a flavour of biddy-bid mixed in to make the tea-leaves go further.

When Mr Cracroft Wilson looked over the section it was empty of children, for Archie, Jim and Emma had gone to join their brothers. It appeared all the tidier for their absence. There was no doubt that his property was improving under her care.

"Clearly you desire to stay, Mrs Phipps," he said. "It's time we drew up an agreement for rent."

"Certainly, sir," she said, "making allowance for our improvements, I have no doubt."

What was the Nabob to do with a woman like that? He said stiffly: "You can discuss that with my lawyer. He'll attend to it. I'm a busy man, Mrs Phipps; and you need not expect to see me very often."

This was perfectly true.

17

A Visitor Unseen

IT was a good summer. The *Garden Queen*, equipped with a
sail from the money for the spring produce, sped up or down
the harbour according to the wind, and had to be rowed only
one way. Real windows were put into the house, and a mangle
for the clothes was set up under a lean-to porch. Still, Mrs
Phipps would spend no money on extra clothes or luxuries,
because they depended for everything on her own skilful
work in the garden. And what would happen to the children if
she should fall ill, or die? They must have some extra way of
making a living.

In the autumn she bought four head of young cattle: two
heifers and two bulls.

The other farmers in the Bay were working in English style with crops of wheat and barley, and ploughed-up pastures sown in English grasses. They paid no attention to the open tussock-land high on the hills. From their experience in Australia, the Phipps family grasped the chance to obtain cheap grazing leases and to run cattle for beef. As there were few fences, the stock were branded; and if they strayed on to someone's property, word was passed to the boys at school. Then Mrs Phipps would go out with Archie and his dog Wally to hunt them back again.

When Jim began school he chummed up with George Bloor, whose father was a farm labourer working for Mr Parsons. One sharp July morning, when even in Governors Bay the frost was white, Jim went down to the beach to look for a frost-fish. George was there before him, with the same idea; but a quite different discovery, an alarming one, sent him rushing up the track, and the two boys almost knocked one another over.

"Jim! Your boat! The *Garden Queen*!"

"What's the matter? Stolen?"

"No –"

"Wrecked?"

"No – it's *sunk*!"

"If it's sunk, it's wrecked, isn't it?"

"No it isn't."

There was only one way to work out this puzzle. Jim raced to the landing-stage and saw, directly below the surface of the falling tide, the charred framework of the dinghy.

"It's burnt!" he said in an awed voice. "Who did that?"

"They did it last night," said George, "because the tide's been over it, see."

"Must've been before midnight."

"But the landing didn't get burnt, only the boat."

"They must have burnt the *Queen*, special!"

"Your mother got any enemies, Jim?"

"It's Jack's boat. We've got to tell him!"

The boys hurried up with their shattering news, and in a few minutes all the Phipps family were there to examine the ruined boat. Jack, in a mixture of grief and fury, threw out questions at everyone. Who had been playing there? Had anyone been around the beach last night? The *Garden Queen* was still there last time water had been brought from the spring. It had happened in the darkness, that was certain. Had anyone been heard prowling then?

"Mother – what do you think?"

For once, there was no answer. Mrs Phipps was not even there. She had left them without saying a word.

"I'll go and ask her," said Mary Ann swiftly.

She was more alarmed at her mother's going than about the boat. Never had Mrs Phipps been dismayed by a trouble, or run short of advice about what to do. Mary Ann hurried into the cottage and found her staring into the fire.

"Mother! Are you ill, Mother?"

"No, Mary Ann, I'm quite well."

"Then why did you come away? Was it so terrible a shock?"

"I think *he* must have come," said Mrs Phipps very slowly.

"Who?"

"Your father."

"You mean," cried Mary Ann, appalled, "our father has come and burnt the *Garden Queen*?"

"Who else would do such a thing to us?"

"That's what none of us can understand."

"If he has come, what will we do, Mary Ann?"

"Mother, *you* are asking *me*?"

Mrs Phipps poked at the fire with a long stick and warmed her hands at the rising flame.

"More than two years we've worked here, at peace with ourselves, and put the hard times behind us, Mary Ann. Oh! I can manage everything without him, but *him* I cannot manage at all. What should we do? Hide? Or go away? Or stay here and wait?"

"Where should we hide; or where could we run to? Why, Mother, we *must* stay! And can you be sure it is him?"

"It would be so *like* him," said Mrs Phipps. "But you are right; we can only wait and see."

"Should we, perhaps, tell the police? Some ruffians might be hereabouts."

Mrs Phipps thought about this.

"I have never been near the police, or the law, since we came here. They might ask questions which I must answer truthfully. What if there are inquiries made for Mrs Small of Berrima?"

"I can hear the children coming," said Mary Ann. "Mother, do go and lie down. I'll tell them you're not well."

"Put the kettle on, and we'll have a cup of tea," said Mrs Phipps, more cheerfully; and she went to the quietness of her bed.

Now it's *my* task, thought Mary Ann, as she set the water to boil; and I must tell the others.

Over the porridge and milk, with hushed voices, they talked of this new fear.

"Let him come," said Bill bluntly. "I'll wager I'm as big as he is, now, and a deal stronger."

"If you strike him, Bill, he'll have the law on you."

"But we can go at him if he goes at us; that's defence," said Jack, who had a score to settle already – and the loss of the *Queen* made it a double score.

"We could stack a lot of stones inside, and bolt the door," said Jim.

"You'd most likely pitch your stone at poor George Bloor," said Mary Ann, scorning this idea too.

Emma, who was four years old now but did not remember her father, broke up the argument by bursting into tears. All this talk of bolting doors and fighting people and a scarifying stranger was too hard to understand. "You mustn't hurt George Bloor!" she wailed.

The boys burst out laughing in spite of themselves; which made Emma cry all the harder, and Mary Ann had to take her up and comfort her. In the midst of the confusion, Mrs Phipps appeared again. She had recovered her usual calmness, and was smiling.

"Now hush, Emma, my dear! We're foolish to be afraid. Nothing bad will happen to us if we keep together! We'll ask God to protect us."

The children were silent as she said a short prayer. Then Archie said:

"Mother, what *will* we do if somebody comes?"

"You will come inside the house straightaway; or, if you're on your way from school, you'll hurry away and not speak. Make haste, now! Goodness, look at the time!"

Bill, who had passed seventeen, was finished with schooling. When his brothers had gone, Mrs Phipps said:

"You must walk to Lyttelton, Bill, and ask the shipwrights about another boat, and let me know the price."

"Is there enough money, Mother?"

"I was saving it to buy more cattle; but the boat has to come first."

"They'll ask me what's happened to the *Garden Queen*. What will I say?"

"That there's been a mishap. Nothing more. I don't want the police hereabouts."

"Are you sure it's safe for him to go?" broke in Mary Ann. She was not sure if she was relieved that her mother had taken charge again, or alarmed at this recklessness. Mrs Phipps answered with a firmness that no one dared question:

"We are in the Lord's hands. I don't give my trust and take it away again!"

Soon Mrs Phipps was working outside as usual, pruning the fruit trees. Bill went to Jack's bunk and drew out, from the groove between the rail and the wall, his brother's latest handiwork – a stock-whip. Long and strong, it would protect him better than a prayer, he told himself.

However, he saw nothing unusual on the way to Lyttelton. At the shipwright's he had the luck to meet a sailor from the last ship to arrive from Australia. Bill got him talking about the passengers and soon was sure that Stephen Small could not possibly have been among them. Of course, he could easily have come by some other way, through Wellington or Nelson; he could even have spent months in the North Island – but Bill felt heartened by this talk. As for the stockwhip, people chaffed him for carrying it and he brightened up his long walk home by flicking seed-heads from the tussocks.

That night the doors on the cottage were bolted. Next morning Bill and Jack went out early to examine the garden and the tracks. There had been another frost, and any footprints would have stood out clearly: but there were none. The daily round began as usual.

In the middle of the morning Emma came racing to her mother where she worked among the fruit trees.

"Somebody's coming! Somebody's coming!"

"Run in to Mary Ann," commanded Mrs Phipps – as if Emma needed telling. She was at the door before her mother had gone ten steps, and come face to face with George Bloor's father.

"Why, you gave me a start, Mr Bloor!"

"Beg pardon, Mrs Phipps, I'm sure. I came about the boat – they told me you had interference!"

"Yes? What have you heard, then?"

"Only what George told me – that he found the boat burnt at the water's edge."

So the story's out, thought Mrs Phipps to herself. She had warned her own boys not to talk but she could not check young George. Mr Bloor went on:

"I'm thinking there's larrikins in these parts. Mr Hodgson lost three pigs, three fine young 'uns he did, with the pen broke down so it couldn't've been no accident. There's tools gone from Mr Dobbs's barn."

"But why should they burn our boat? If they were thieving, they'd more likely set it adrift."

"They could've stole it, and returned it, and burnt it to destroy some evidence, maybe? Did Bill tell the police yesterday?"

"No," said Mrs Phipps.

"No? Mr Hodgson's been up about them pigs and they'll come around asking. You'll not mind me telling about the boat, in case it's all one crime?"

All one crime!

With these three words Mr Bloor, without knowing it, swept a great load from Mrs Phipps's shoulders. Suddenly she felt sure that the stranger was *not* Stephen Small. A brutal husband and father he might be, but he was no criminal. It must have been some "ruffian" as Mary Ann had said; and she was not in the least afraid of any ruffian.

"Yes, Mr Bloor, to be sure," she said. "A woman doesn't always understand these things."

Mr Bloor felt flattered by this remark. "I'm ready to help anyways I can," he said warmly.

To the children, the thought of thieves was only a trifle less alarming than the thought of their father; and so the doors were bolted again that night. But as the week went by, the panic appeared silly. Emma, who had stayed close to the cottage all day, went down to the beach to play; and in the evenings, as they gathered around the fire, Mrs Phipps told stories and sang songs as gaily as ever. Only she hated taking eleven pounds from her savings to buy a new boat, with a sail. She could never feel the same about the *Phoenix* as she did about the *Garden Queen*, which had been found for her out of the gratitude and kindness of her Maori neighbours.

Nobody ever found Mr Hodgson's pigs, or Mr Dobbs's tools, or solved the mystery of the burnt boat. New Zealand was a large empty country where a thief might easily melt away, and settle down with his stolen goods to live like an honest man. Besides, soon there was a fresh excitement.

18

The Call of the Gold

ONE Saturday afternoon in July, when Bill had been helping Mr Beechey with some fencing, he arrived home unexpectedly with the *Lyttelton Times* screwed up in his hand. Mrs Phipps was sorting seeds on the kitchen table. "What brings you, Bill?" she said in alarm. Bill did not answer, but unscrewed his newspaper and, spreading it out on top of the seeds, he pointed to an advertisement topped with a small engraving of a ship.

STEAM TO THE TUAPEKA GOLDFIELDS

The Powerful Paddle Steamer *Prince Albert*, Robt. Spence, Master, will leave the Government Wharf on Monday next (wind and weather permitting), at 4 o'clock p.m., direct for Dunedin Jetty.

For freight or passage, apply to E. A. Hargreaves, Norwich Quay.

"I'm going, Mother!" said Bill. "I'm off to get my passage before the *Prince Albert*'s crowded out."

"Gold talk!" said Mrs Phipps. "It's been coming out of Otago for months."

"*This* is the real thing! Listen." Bill opened the paper and read the news of Gabriel's Gully. "Mr Millar's party of seven obtained in one day 38 ounces and a few pennyweights, and in nine days the total amount obtained by the same party was 127 ounces. Mr Gabriel Read's party sent in 168½ ounces!" He emphasized all the figures triumphantly. "I'm rolling my swag to be down among the first."

"I don't hear you asking my permission," said Mrs Phipps sharply.

"I'm seventeen, going on eighteen, and I'm not such a fool as to throw away a chance like this! I told Mr Beechey I'll not be a farm labourer all my days."

"When?"

"When I saw the paper at his place."

"You don't give yourself long to think."

"I've thought about it for years, Mother – only waiting for the chance!"

Mrs Phipps could not deny this.

"Have you thought of the money?" she asked.

"I won't need much! Only a washing dish, and a pick and shovel, and a roll of blankets, and a quid or two to get started – so long as I'm down with the first."

"They'll be in from Dunedin before you."

"Mother – give me the money and let me go!"

All of his wages had been handed in, week after week, except for the last few shillings from Mr Beechey which he had now in his pocket. That was the way Mrs Phipps managed the money for all the family.

"I had meant to buy more calves," she said.

"There'll always be calves but there won't always be gold."

"A gold rush makes more fools than it makes fortunes!"

Bill lost patience altogether.

"There's a ship sailing in the morning, and I'm going – if I have to steal the money!"

"You won't have to steal it. I'll give it to you – but there won't be any more where that comes from, Bill. Once you're away, you'll manage on your own."

"Manage!" cried Bill, jubilant as he saw a wide, beautiful world open up in his imagination. "Two weeks, and I'll be rolling in it! I'll be hanging the nuggets on my gold watch-chain, and bringing home silk dresses for you, Mother!"

"And what would I do with a silk dress, Bill? Wear it to clean out the fowl-run? Take that newspaper off the table, you're messing all my seeds up."

She went on with her work, while Bill took the new boat, the *Phoenix*, and went off to Lyttelton to book his passage and buy his prospector's gear.

For weeks afterwards, the newspapers printed encouraging news about Gabriel's Gully and the Tuapeka Diggings. A scrawly letter arrived from Bill to say that he had found a good mate and they were already working on "tucker ground" – which meant they were panning enough gold to keep themselves in food. At any moment, as they dug deeper and wider, they would make that lucky strike. But Bill was not much of a letter-writer and no other news arrived.

One Sunday in spring, Mary Ann left early for church with her arms full of bluebells and stocks to decorate the altar. The cob hut was still being used for services, although the new St Cuthbert's, built by voluntary labour, was growing near to completion. The children followed later, leaving Mrs Phipps to cook the Sunday dinner. Everything was ready when Emma and Jim came running home ahead of the others, singing "All things bright and beautiful" at the tops of their voices. Emma could sing proper tunes now and no longer made up her own songs with one word at a time. Archie and Jack followed; but there was no sign of Mary Ann.

"She was talking to people," was all the children could say.

It was not Mrs Phipps's way to have a good meal spoiled. She dished up the meat and vegetables, and then the "spotty Dick", putting Mary Ann's share to the side of the fire, and wondering all the time what could possibly have kept the girl. When the meal was over she told the boys to attend to the dishes, and set out to find her.

Following a hunch, she looked into a ferny nook where Mary Ann liked to go when they were out walking; and there she was, sitting on a log with little pieces of leaves and flowers crumbled over her lap. She was so still that a bush-robin pecked at her boot.

"What is the matter, Mary Ann?" asked Mrs Phipps, gently putting an arm around her shoulders.

The girl was too miserable even to cry, but she grasped her mother's hands and held them tight; and after a time the story came out – an old, familiar story.

Mary Ann was loyal and loving, and if she were often sharp

with her brothers and sister it was because she was covering her great disappointment about the young man whom she could not follow from Sydney to England. Now at last there had appeared another. He had a good education and charming manners; and they had met often enough at church, or at Mrs Dyer's place. But today in the gossip that followed the service, from which he was absent, it came out that he had become engaged to a young lady in Christchurch – also of good education and charming manners.

"And I am a nobody," stammered Mary Ann, "with no mansion at home in England, and I've never been to school, and I'm awkward in company, and my words don't come out right when I speak!"

"Don't take on so," said Mrs Phipps soothingly, but Mary Ann went on:

"It was the same before. *They* have 'people' in England, but *we* are no better than labourers without even a father, alive or dead!"

She had touched on the point so sore that Mrs Phipps herself never mentioned it. While the other settlers spoke often of "Home" and looked eagerly for letters when the ships came in, nothing arrived for the Phipps family except an occasional note from Mrs McCracken. Afraid of some mistake or misunderstanding, Mrs Phipps herself had never written to friends or relatives in London; and the children knew they must say nothing about "Mr Phipps". It was only known that they had lived in Australia; and for all anyone knew, they might have had connections with the convicts. Class distinctions were strong in early Canterbury. Many a young man would hesitate before courting a girl who could have convict blood.

"There'll be others, my dear," said Mrs Phipps. "You are so excellent a cook and housekeeper! One day a gentleman will see that these virtues are worth more than family and position. Try to believe in yourself, Mary Ann!"

"No!" cried Mary Ann. "I shall never dare look at any man again!"

She meant it. But "a trouble shared is a trouble halved", and after that she pulled herself together and went home. Sitting in the sunshine with her plateful of "spotty Dick" she comforted herself with the knowledge that her own family would stand by her, even though she would never marry.

The boys and Emma understood very little of this trouble, and yet it filled up the spaces in the household that seemed empty without Bill. They all went out of their way to be kind. This was not easy, for on some days Mary Ann went about her work without a word to anyone, and on other days she broke into fits of temper for no apparent reason.

On one of her "edgy" days, Jim was scolded for being under her feet, when the truth was he had nothing to do. It was a Saturday and there was no school. Mrs Phipps was in Lyttelton with Jack and Emma, selling flowers; while Archie had gone up the hills with Wally to look over the cattle. So Jim took a billy and went looking for George Bloor to go to the Pinnacle. After catching six crabs without trouble, they started a fire going on the beach to boil them up.

George looked up from his stoking with a surprised giggle.

"Did you put a scarecrow up in the flax?" he said.

"What?" said Jim. "What you talking about?"

"Look there – it moves!" roared George.

Jim stared. Through the low flax and fern sloping into the gully, a man was coming down. He certainly made queer

progress, standing up, bending over, catching at flax-stalks, disappearing, appearing again.

"Might be after pigs," said Jim.

"Haw! No pigs there, and where's his gun?"

"P'raps he's lost?" Jim suggested uneasily.

"He's drunk more likely! And anyway he's not lost if he can see *us*!"

Jim poked some more sticks into the fire and took another look. "He's got wild-looking whiskers!" he said, ready for a laugh with George; but the moment he said it he remembered their fear, only a few months ago, of "a stranger". The fear stirred him now, and anxiously he said: "D'you think he's very *old*?"

"Old as the hills, to grow all that bush on his face!"

George could laugh, and Jim joined in to make himself feel better, for he dared not say that he was quivering inside. The stranger disappeared into the gully and the boys, turning to their fire, saw that the water was boiling. They dropped in three of the crabs and straightened up – just in time to confront the man who staggered out of the bushes looking more like a scarecrow than ever. He was thin and gaunt, and his shirt and trousers were almost falling apart.

"Jim!" came a familiar voice.

"Bill! It's Bill!"

The "stranger" reeled and sank down on the bank.

"Fetch me something to eat and drink, Jim!" he moaned.

Suddenly Jim felt shy and awkward. This new arrival was a brother and a stranger, all at once – a boy when he left home, and they'd taken him for a man! "What d'you want to eat?" he asked.

"Anything. And milk. 'Specially milk."

Jim became charged with importance. "You look after him, George!" He ran home, hoping that Mary Ann's sharp mood had simmered down; and luckily it had. Within ten minutes she had come with him, carrying milk, fruit, a new-made loaf, butter and cheese and jam. "You wouldn't know him," Jim was saying. "We thought he was drunk." And indeed Mary Ann would not have recognized her brother until she looked into his eyes, for he was quite silent now.

A pannikin of milk disappeared down Bill's throat. The sweet-smelling, warm bread was snatched from her hands before she could spread the butter properly. He ate like a starved animal until he was satisfied. Then he rubbed his dry, grimed hands in the sand to clean them.

"Where's Mother?"

"In Lyttelton, with Jack and Emma. Archie's up the hills."

"That's lucky. I should clean myself up."

"Bill, where are your things?"

"My things? I sold them. Except the blankets – and they rolled over a cliff somewhere. I don't know where. I can't remember!" he said wildly, almost shouting.

"You're home now," she said quietly. "You can tell me everything, for Mother will ask. You sold your things to buy food?"

"To keep digging. Any moment our luck might change."

"And it didn't?"

"If we could've kept on..." he trailed off.

"There must always be an end, Bill." Mary Ann was thinking of her own trouble as much as his; but he did not know this. And now Jim, overcome with curiosity, took a turn.

"How far did you walk?"

"All the way."

"Did you – honest? How long?"

"Three weeks. A day over."

"Thought you had a mate."

"He stayed in Dunedin."

"What did you live on, then?"

"Eels and wekas; when I could catch them."

Now George broke in. "What did you catch them with?" he put in. "And how did you cook them?"

The answer was disappointing.

"I just ate them," said Bill.

Only Mary Ann grasped what he meant. He must have eaten them raw! Poor, desperate Bill! She said firmly:

"Boys, go away and don't ask so many questions! Can't you see he's worn out? Come on, Bill – there's hot water in the kettle. We'll smarten you up before Mother gets home. Jim, you can stop here with your crabs."

"Crabs?" said Bill, in a queer sort of way.

Mary Ann had to help him up, and he walked slowly, leaning on her and not even looking ashamed to do so. Jim and George watched him going and marvelled.

"He didn't even notice the crabs!" said Jim.

"You forgot them yourself," scoffed George. "The fire's out, and the live ones got away."

Jim peeped into the billy. "Anyway, there's three good ones. We could save one for Bill," he said, feeling very noble and generous and full of pity for his ruined brother.

19

The Vanishing Cattle

BILL did not want to talk about the Otago diggings. After a
few days, when his strength had returned, he went quietly out
to see what work he could find; but Mr Beechey had another
man in his place and the harvest was over. It was some time
before he found work on the roads.

But nobody was allowed to think that Bill had been cured
of the gold fever. He was ready to admit that he and his mate
had been green; they were "new chums"; but the clever ones
had made fortunes and next time he would be among the clever
ones himself. One day he heard Emma singing the popular
jingle:

Gold, gold, fine bright gold!
Wangapeka, Tuapeka, bright red gold!

He thought she was teasing him and poor Emma, who had no idea that Tuapeka was the place of Bill's failure, received a hiding before her mother could rescue her.

Although discoveries were made in Central Otago, Bill made no effort to make good his boasting. He had had enough of those dry, harsh hills. There was gold west of Nelson too, but the Canterbury papers did not encourage any interest in this rival province. They wanted gold to be found in their own part of the country. Unluckily the only finds were in "West Canterbury", which was later named Westland. That, too, was a place for only the toughest people. No one went there except for Maoris and a few explorers, surveyors and prospectors. They wrote of steep mountains, swift and dangerous rivers, bush too dense to squeeze through, and rain, rain, rain, rain. Men were drowned in the rivers and lakes, while others came back as starved and exhausted as Bill had been. And for all that they found only a few grains of gold.

So Bill stayed at home and worked for his living, sometimes in their own garden but more often as a labourer. Jack, who had finished school too, gave nearly all his time to the boat. The *Phoenix* was busy on most days of the week with all sorts of commissions for transporting goods. People in Lyttelton were becoming interested in picnic trips, so Jack saved his money and bought a cutter which could be hired as a pleasure boat. Sometimes he travelled round to the Peninsula Bays which were being opened up for timber, or took wheat to Akaroa to be ground. New settlers were coming in, and old farms were being extended. Mr Dyer himself, with a young family to think of, moved to a larger property on the other side of the Beecheys.

Among the attractions of Governors Bay was Mrs Phipps's own garden. There was a sure sale for everything she grew; and people liked to come in person to admire the masses of gay flowers or to choose fruit for themselves.

More grazing leases were bought, the cattle herd grew, and Archie – who had completed school by the age of thirteen – was always busy with Wally at his heels. It was a steady, busy and generally happy life for the family.

Then in August 1864, three years after the Otago goldrush had begun, exciting news broke in Canterbury.

On the other side of the snowy ranges, from the banks of a river flowing into the Teremakau, one Albert Hunt sent a sample of gold to Christchurch. And he wrote that he "could get the colour in any place", that he had panned 38 ounces already and that a party of four might make £150 in a week.

Bill read this letter in the *Lyttelton Times* over and over again, as he had once read the *Otago News*, but this time the phrase that circled round and round in his mind was this: "I can get the colour *in any place*." In any place! All that coastline, all those numberless rivers and streams; and there was gold in any place!

Bill did not wait for any more information; and his mother did not waste time trying to stop him. He bought a new pick, shovel, dish and blanket-roll and set off by the only route that was open – the old Maori route over Harper's Pass, known in those days as the Hurunui Saddle.

This time, Bill was among the few hundred men who went ahead of the main goldrushes. Over several months, people in Christchurch were doubtful about Albert Hunt's claims; and as for the prospectors, they were not very anxious to tell. In any case they could send no letters home unless they met up with some travelling party or a sea-captain to carry them.

Christmas came and went without any word from Bill.

In February there was another burst of news. A ship had arrived in Nelson with about two thousand pounds' worth of gold, all dug in that wild coast!

Now the people of Canterbury did take notice. Why, this was Canterbury territory; and they should be raking in the profits, not letting them go to Nelson! They would have to build a road to the West, over the shorter route of Arthur's Pass. But this would take months, and who could wait for that? Certainly not the diggers! Shiploads left for the West Coast from Dunedin, Nelson, Melbourne and Lyttelton; and thousands of men tramped overland by the old Hurunui Saddle.

At this time George Bloor made another discovery that shocked the Phipps family out of their quiet life.

Very early one warm morning he was awakened by the howling of his dog. From the direction of the sound he guessed that the dog was off the chain and this was strictly forbidden. To save himself from a hiding by his father, George crept out of bed to tie the dog up again.

The first glow of dawn was mingled with the moonlight to show George what had aroused the dog. Along the road came two men, with swags on their backs, one of them carrying a gun. Between them went eight bullocks.

"Hello!" said one of the men with a start, as George came out of the shadows to hold his dog. "What's this – what you prowling about for, in the night?"

"I came to get *him*," said George, very scared. "He ought to be on the chain."

"Well, you chain him and get back to bed before you get yourself in trouble!"

One of the bullocks brushed close to George and he found himself staring at a familiar brand mark. Without stopping to think he burst out:

"You got Archie Phipps's cattle!"

"Eh?" The man was caught off guard, but his mate said smoothly:

"Yes, we bought 'em last night. Paid Archie good money for 'em, we did, so as to make an early start this morning."

George said no more, for his mouth was quite dry with fear. The scared feeling stayed with him all day and he said nothing to his family – in any case he couldn't admit that the dog was loose. He was not a quick thinker and it took him a long time to sort out the truth in this strange conversation.

He had spoken up, himself, about Archie Phipps's cattle. And the man had answered that he paid Archie for them. But, if he'd paid anyone, it would not have been Archie, but Mrs Phipps! Perhaps the men did not know that Archie was a boy only two years older than George himself. They must be cattle thieves! There was no doubt about it.

Now, after another worrying night, George went looking for Archie. It took him a while to find him, because he did not want to go directly to Mrs Phipps. By the time the news was out, the men had nearly two days' start.

There was no such slowness about Mrs Phipps. Although it was late in the afternoon she set off on foot to Cashmere, over the now completed road, to inquire if the bullocks had been seen. Yes, the shepherds told her, they had been driven in the direction of Riccarton and without doubt up the North Road. No one had stopped them, believing the cattle to be honestly bought. The men were probably diggers, aiming to make a few extra pounds by taking fresh meat on the hoof; for cattle were fetching a fabulous price on the West Coast.

Mrs Phipps strode home in the summer dusk. The waters of the harbour lay softly like dark-blue silk, and the houses of Governors Bay nestled cosily into the hills beneath her, but her thoughts were angry and determined. As she came down towards her own home, she found Archie and Jim wandering up to meet her. Archie was looking very downcast about their loss.

"Are you going to get them back, Mother?"

"No, Archie!" Her tone was surprisingly cheerful. "We will not waste time chasing after what is gone. Why shouldn't we follow their example?"

"*You're* not going to steal cattle!" exclaimed Jim.

"Shan't I, Jim? We could soon make up for what's lost!"

"No," said Jim flatly. "You wouldn't."

"Well then, we shall steal our own before anyone else does. Those men know where the profits are. Why shouldn't we have our share too?"

"Where have they gone, Mother?" asked Archie.

"Yes – where?" echoed Jim.

"To the goldfields! There's a great hunger for beef, they tell me, and the first to come have the pick of the market; and a beast that'd fetch us seven pounds in Lyttelton will bring four and five times more over there. We'll have them down from the hills tomorrow, boys, for there's more to be done on the goldfields than fossicking for gold!"

20

The Diggers' Road

WITHIN two days, the cattle were mustered and ready to
start, with Wally standing guard to see that they did not stray.
Although Archie had never succeeded in justifying the full
name "Wallaby" by teaching his dog to jump, he had trained
up a splendid worker. There were twenty-five young bullocks,
eight cows, and a tough old pack-bullock who was brought
down to the house and loaded with supplies – a tent, billies,
blankets, a little warm clothing, matches and food.

"Will you see Bill over there, Mother? Will you look for
him?" they all wanted to know. And really it was her dearest
wish that they might find him; but she had to say that it was
only a small chance – the goldfields ran along the coast for
nearly a hundred miles.

Only Archie was to go with her. Mary Ann had charge of

the house. Jim, who had left school now, would help Jack to harvest the fruit and vegetables and take them to be sold. Only seven-year-old Emma minded being left; and she minded so much that she clung all day at her mother's side, getting in the way of the preparations.

Mrs Phipps filled a basket with eggs, just big enough for Emma to carry, and herself took a freshly-killed rooster for a quick visit to Rapaki. That she should go now, when everything was in such a whirl, was a mystery to the others. Ever since the women had come to take refuge from the storm, there had been frequent comings and goings between Rapaki and the Phipps's cottage. Maori gratitude was long-lived, and from time to time little gifts were sent over. Mrs Phipps had her independent ways as well, and liked to return the compliment sometimes. But why *now*?

On the way, Emma had her mother all to herself. She felt important with her basket to carry; and she forgot her tears and joined in when Mrs Phipps began to sing funny verses like this one:

> "The man in the wilderness asked of me,
> How many strawberries grow in the sea?
> I answered him as I thought good,
> As many red herrings as grow in the wood!"

Nowadays Emma could do more than sing – she could whistle, and a bright little refrain followed the last line and startled a tomtit right off his branch. Mrs Phipps went on:

> "Laugh and the world laughs with you,
> Weep and you're weeping alone,
> Prosper and give and they'll let you live
> But fail, and you're on your own."

By the time they returned home, Emma was whistling gaily all round the place. She was going to look after the hens, she said, and take the spare eggs to Rapaki each week so that her mother wouldn't worry while she was away.

So, with stout boots on their feet and cheerful farewells behind them, Mrs Phipps and Archie set out over Dyer's Pass and through Riccarton, to reach the diggers' road.

In the village of Kaiapoi, twelve miles north of Christchurch, the people found it hard to get their day's work done. As soon as the first voice could be heard shouting, "Here come the diggers!", windows would fly open, shopkeepers would follow their customers to the doors, and men would leave the hotel bar with their foaming tankards in their hands. Sometimes the diggers came in twos and threes, sometimes as many as fifty at a time. It was all the same: there was much joking and back-slapping and hand-shaking as the Kaiapoi people wished them all the fortune in the world – especially if they returned to spend some of the money in Kaiapoi.

On this March morning there appeared a more unusual sight. Not that there was anything unusual about a mob of cattle – or even a loaded pack-bullock; but with these, there walked a little women of middle age, a boy of fifteen, and a large tawny collie dog; and no man at all! The woman's clothes were neat, and she wore lace at her throat, but her skirt was shortened above the ankle and her boots were as sturdy as a man's. At the baker's, she went in to ask for fresh bread.

"And where be you taking your stock, madam?" asked the baker politely.

"To the diggings," she said. "The Teremakau."

The baker leaned over his counter, speaking confidentially,

although every word could be followed by the knot of people gathering around the door.

"The 'terrible Cow' they calls that river! Did they tell you what like o' country it is? Times they come back through here, chest and throat all knocked up, not a penny to pay for the bread nor a hand steady enough to hold it!"

"I know," she said. "I'm well acquainted and well prepared."

"It'll be raining torrents over there, seeing it's nor'west here!" said a man standing by.

"Then likely it'll be over before we get there."

"It'll make mud-pools up to your neck, and flood all the rivers!"

"I'm well prepared," repeated Mrs Phipps, smiling.

"Good luck to you, madam," said the baker, "and may we have your custom on your return? You'll be glad of fresh bread by then, I'll warrant."

"I'll be calling," she assured him gaily, and the little crowd parted for her to go out, all wishing her well.

Out in the street, Archie and Wally were the centre of a crowd of boys.

"Where're you taking them cattle?" asked the foremost one.

"To the diggings," said Archie.

"Over the snowy ranges? Ain't you got no father – just you and your mother?"

"That's right."

"Garn! You'll get bogged in the mud."

Other boys chimed in:

"You got to swim the rivers, d'ye know? Can those cows swim?"

"The dead 'uns will make good tucker for your dog!"

"Got your panning dish?"

"They get you drunk in them grog-shanties!"

All this was backed up with so many laughs and shouts that Archie couldn't get a word in, but the next question was followed by a serious silence.

"What'll you do, if robbers stick your mother up?"

"I've got a knife," said Archie calmly.

"Show us, show us!"

Archie unsheathed his bowie-knife and let them feel its keen point and blade. One boy thrust out another question:

"And what'll your mother do if robbers stick *you* up?"

"She's got a knife the same as that one!"

This brought a burst of cheering; and the boys stood back in respectful awe as Mrs Phipps came out of the baker's shop with her bread to load on to the pack-bullock. Wally, who was peacefully dozing, was roused and the mob moved noisily away up the road.

They were near to the end of their second day out from home. Clouds of dust rolled with the nor'wester over the tussock plains, fit to choke cattle and drovers together. On they went until they came to a small clear stream, where Mrs Phipps and Archie could cool themselves, and the mob be rested.

"What were the boys saying?" asked Mrs Phipps.

"That we'd be sure to get bogged, or drowned – us or the cattle!" Archie grinned. "And why hadn't we got a father with us, and what if we were stuck up by robbers?"

"We'll show them!" his mother laughed. "We're better without a man. There's one pitfall we'll miss."

"What's that?"

"The grog! And besides – why do you think I went to Rapaki, Archie?"

"To take fowls and eggs, and get Emma happy."

"Yes – and to talk to the men that know this trail! *They* were going through those mountains before gold was ever heard of, or bullocks, or boots for that matter. They do say that whenever a pakeha will take the Maori advice, he comes to no harm in the ranges."

"They've got kinsmen over there," said Archie. "I've heard them talk about it."

"Yes, they're all Ngai-Tahu... Oh, it'll be fun coming back through Kaiapoi. Bogged or drowned or stuck up by robbers, is it? We shall see!"

2I

Encounter in the Darkness

IT took five days to pass through the tussock country, through Waipara and the Weka Pass and the Waikari Basin. Mrs Phipps did not want to hurry the cattle, but to give them good grazing for as long as was possible. Camping places were well marked by those who had gone before them; and soon they were experts at pitching the tent and making comfortable beds on the hard ground.

The road was never empty. Coaches, taking the better-off prospectors with them, rolled past amid noisy cheers. Horsemen and foot-travellers were continually pressing past the slow-moving cattle. But all this speed came to a stop when the road ended at the entrance to the Waitohi Gorge.

Here there was a small settlement: a rough-looking accommodation house, a grog-shanty, and a store with hardly any goods to offer. Abandoned waggons lay about, for they were less valuable than the gold which their owners expected to find at the other end of the trail.

People gathered round Archie and his mother to offer good advice.

"You keep those cattle mighty quiet going through the Gorge, or you'll have 'em bolting up the bush, or toppled in the river afore you can wink!" said a man.

"And don't let that dog go barking at their heels," said another.

"Wally's trained," Archie answered proudly. "He won't bark."

The track led up the Waitohi into a smaller tributary and over a low saddle to the Hurunui valley. They were a hundred feet above the river on a path only wide enough to go single-file, where the cattle must not be alarmed by anything, such as men and horses trying to pass in a hurry. Mrs Phipps took the lead with the pack-bullock, while Archie and Wally came last. In this way, other travellers could be politely warned of the size of the mob, and where possible the bullocks could be turned into a wider space for a spell.

This plan worked well. After about three miles of the main gorge, they entered the tributary and, crossing and re-crossing the stream about twenty times, they came to the saddle. At some time there had been a bush fire, for there were burnt stumps of great trees all about, and grass grew on the slopes. Many people had camped on the small flat which lay below.

Clearly, if the cattle should stray it would be impossible to find them all again. From now on the guarding could not be left to Wally alone. Archie and Mrs Phipps had to take turns all night, one watching, one sleeping.

Next morning they were away early into the still more difficult gorge of the Hurunui. Fast and blue flowed the river, between banks so high and narrow that Archie could throw a stone across and hear the crack echo back to him, but he could neither see nor hear it strike the water. River-shags flew screeching by. It was all very beautiful, but often he was too busy to look at anything but the great patches of sticky mud over which the bullocks had to be coaxed. The nor'west rain had done its work here. Sometimes there were shelving patches of rock where a false step would send boy or beast sliding straight down into the rowdy river.

It took all day to cover those eight miles and to come out into a wider valley where a storekeeper had set up in business, selling nothing much except flour, sugar, tea, salt and bacon. By now, damper baked in the camp-fire embers was the main food for Archie and Mrs Phipps, as it was for most foot-travellers.

Next morning, the south branch of the Hurunui had to be crossed just before it joined the north branch which the travellers must follow. Here there was a tent for selling whisky and rum; and the shanty-keeper was doing well, for men liked to warm up their insides before plunging into the icy water which was three feet deep in the middle. Indeed, there was a small mob of bullocks here but no drover to be seen.

"He's kicking up his heels, I daresay," said Mrs Phipps, looking disapprovingly at the tent, "and his cattle looking after themselves. They'll be half-starved when they get to the diggings – if they haven't lost themselves first."

At the ford, she tried out the first piece of advice she had been given by the Maoris. She gave Archie the other end of a stout pole and, holding it before them, keeping side on to the current, they walked across with one careful step placed after another. Of course they were thoroughly wet, but that was something to be taken for granted. As for the cattle, once the leader was across the others followed, with plenty of encouragement from Wally who was allowed to bark as much as he liked.

Lake Taylor, the site of the last sheep-station on the route and the only one in this area of lakes, river-valleys and towering mountains, was another favourite camping-place. Watching his cattle that night, Archie counted the lights of twenty-seven camp fires. George Taylor and his wife, of the Lakes Station, must often have wearied of the many people who came, hungry and sick, looking for help, and of the cattle which grazed where they ran their own sheep. In spite of this their kindness was well known, and Mrs Phipps decided to call on Mrs Taylor. This was a man's country, and a woman must long to talk to a woman, as she did herself.

Mrs Taylor received her in friendly fashion.

"You'd be wise to make a good camp," she said, "for if I'm not mistaken, there's more rain coming. What if it should rain for a week?"

"We can't hold our bullocks," said Mrs Phipps. "Rain or no rain, I mean to get them there in good condition!"

"Then make the most of one dry night, for you never know when the next will be!" was the cheerful comment.

Next day they found the lake shores so swampy that they passed the bodies of several horses which had become bogged. Here again they had to take the greatest of care in keeping the cattle to firm ground. Past lovely Lake Katherine, alongside

great and broad Lake Sumner they went, and into the tall
beech forest.

By this time the rain had indeed come and the daylight was
growing dim. Although this was not the best place, with water
falling from the branches in large, stinging drops, Mrs Phipps
decided to stop as soon as she found enough clear and level
ground to hold the cattle. There was a dry corner under a
bank for the fire, and the tent was secure enough although
perched over stones and sodden leaves. Mrs Phipps made a hot
supper of rice and bacon; and then, just as they made ready for
the night, she found that one of the cows was missing.

"I'll find her, Mother," said Archie. "It's my turn for
early watch, and anyway I'm needing some wekas for dog
tucker."

The wekas were not hard to find. They were calling from
everywhere around, and often the sound was joined by the
shrill cries of the kiwi, but these were not daring enough to
show themselves. Archie kept on the move even when it was
quite dark and too risky to go far afield looking for the cow.
He wanted to be sure that none of the others joined her; and
besides it was the only way to keep warm.

But before it was time to rouse his mother to take her turn,
he came to the tent and wakened here.

"Mother! There's someone about!"

She sat up, feeling the sodden ground ooze beneath her, and
brushed back her hair which was plaited for the night.

"Someone? Who, Archie?"

"I can hear a man snoring, or grunting – I don't know
what."

"Are you sure? A weka, or some bird –"

"No, it's not. Do come, Mother!"

She reached for her cloak. Everything felt sodden and her boots were thick with mud which struck cold against her feet. As they stumbled through the trees the low bushes whipped against their faces, but at least in this beech forest there were no great tangles of supplejack.

"Listen," whispered Archie.

A long shrill call came, answered by another.

"Kiwis!" she said.

"No – listen!"

There were only the crackling, clicking, dripping noises of the bush.

"I'm sure it was here," said Archie. "Let's try this way."

They edged along a log heavy with filmy ferns, and Archie trod on a stick which cracked like a pistol-shot. At once, almost at their feet, came a deep moaning and a thick, mumbled voice:

"Who'sh that?"

"He's hurt!" cried Mrs Phipps.

The sound of a woman's voice in that drenched wilderness would have stirred a dying man. However, this man wasn't dying. His one companion – his whisky bottle – had failed him and left him helpless in the mud.

"Help him up, Archie, and we'll walk him to the tent."

"I can walk with the nexsht man. Who'sh that? Who'sh that?" complained the stranger.

"What if he's dangerous?" whispered Archie.

"Stuff! He's helpless, not dangerous. Come, we'll drag him to the fire."

They did this, to the tune of many grunts and feeble yells. The sticks which had been laid close to the glow to dry out for the morning were pushed into the fire which was soon blazing brightly. The man was propped against the bank where he watched the steam rising from his own clothes.

"You take your rest now, Archie," said Mrs Phipps.

"What if you need me?" Archie fingered his bowie-knife and looked suspiciously at their guest; but his mother only laughed.

"He's not dangerous! Off you go now!"

Archie crept gratefully into the tent, pulled off his boots, rolled up in the damp blankets and went to sleep.

The rain was still falling, but very gently. Mrs Phipps put the billy on the fire and brewed strong, sweet tea. This she cooled enough to be sure it could not scald the man, and made him drink it, ignoring his mumbled demands for whisky. Then she found what was left of the rice, and warmed it spoonful by spoonful. The man ate greedily. At last he slid awkwardly so close to the fire that she had to rake the embers away from him, and with noisy snoring he fell asleep.

It was morning before the stranger was fit for conversation. When he heard that the Lakes Station was only half a day's walking distance, he tried his legs and declared that he could easily get there by himself. Mrs Phipps questioned him:

"You're a prospector – going home?"

"Yes, thank you kindly, ma'am."

"Where's your mate?"

"Drownded!"

"Oh, what a misfortune! Where did this happen?"

"In the 'terrible Cow'. I tried to save him – it waren't no use. There's more bones than stones in that river."

Archie shivered, but said nothing, and Mrs Phipps pressed on.

"No luck with the gold?"

"We got a little; and that's all gone down the river with

him. We was packing up anyway. It's the rain that got us beat. The whisky's all gone; only thing what keeps your insides dry. The rain goes right through otherwise."

"Stuff!" said Mrs Phipps. "What you need is some good food inside you, and we've given you a morsel of that."

"Thank you kindly, ma'am."

"We'll set you on your way, but first, tell me. Did you meet anyone over there by the name of Phipps? Bill Phipps?"

"Bills by the dozen. Scores of 'em. Hundreds of 'em. What name did you say, ma'am?"

"Bill Phipps."

"Not that I heard tell of. You going to join their party, you and the boy here? You got a right recipe for luck, eh, boy?"

Archie looked across at Wally and the bullocks, and the thought flashed across his mind that *they* never made such fools of themselves.

"No," he said quietly. "We're drovers."

"Good for you, matey. Stick to it. Stick to the beef, I say!"

Mrs Phipps and Archie watched him go – another wrecked man who would be pleading for the contents of Mrs Taylor's cupboards; and both of them were thinking of how Bill had come home from the Otago goldfields, as parched and dry, inside and out, as this man was wet.

"Where do you think Bill is now?" Archie burst out.

"Not like that, I hope," said Mrs Phipps grimly.

The lost cow had not re-appeared. It was not much use, now, looking for her; and with thirty-three beasts they set off again up the valley.

22

Mates on the Track

Two damp days were taken up in reaching the Saddle. For the last three miles the Hurunui, which ran faster as it became smaller, had to be crossed more than thirty times, with the cattle sometimes coaxed and sometimes driven and sometimes having to be hunted back from the bush. The tall beech forest gave way to sub-alpine scrub and then to open heath where, on a whirr of wings, the keas descended. Where the Hurunui took its source from foaming torrents pouring down a mountain-side, there stood a slab hut.

Provisions could be bought here, though it could hardly be called a store. "I should have to be very hungry before I bought any of *that* flour," Mrs Phipps said to Archie, shuddering at the great black rats which bounded over the sacks in the full light of day. But the storekeeper had a good fire going and he welcomed them in, to warm and dry themselves and to listen to gold-talk.

"Weather's clearing, I think, missus," he said, "but you'll be wet all the same, in and out of the rivers. You got someone watching out for you?"

"I've a son on the diggings: Bill Phipps. You haven't heard of him?"

"Can't say as I have. You can't keep tabs on 'em. You hear they're in one place, and when you get there they've rushed off after some other strike fifty miles away. You'll be lucky if you see hide or hair of him."

Archie, who could see no sense in getting dry when he'd be wet again within half an hour, stood outside, watching the keas. These cheeky green parrots reminded him of the boys at Kaiapoi, flocking round and staring curiously, with cocked heads, and scratching their toes on the ground. The difference was that they couldn't ask their questions about why human beings made such crazy journeys.

Next came the climb to the Hurunui Saddle itself.

Swampy patches between the snowgrass had been churned by passing feet and hooves into pools of slush full of roots and stones. Terrified and trembling, the cattle picked their way through, trying to find firm ground but often sinking down to their knees; and much time had to be given to helping them out again. When they had descended through stony ground and stunted shrubs into the Teremakau, the poor beasts found travel even more terrifying. The stream, still quite small, surged down a deep gully so cluttered with boulders that there was often only just enough room for a bullock to be squeezed through. Sometimes they could be coaxed and sometimes they had to be forced, and it was not easy for Archie or Mrs Phipps to keep a footing against the force of the current. Fallen trees had to be clambered over or under. One moment they would be deep in mud, the next they would be waist-deep in icy water.

"At least it cleans me up," said Mrs Phipps as she wrung the water from her skirt and remembered oddly how Mary Ann had complained of her long dress, because of the heat, on the road from Berrima.

Archie could not hear her, because he was far ahead and out of sight, and in any case the river was too rowdy for conversation. He was alarmed to see two men coming up: would they frighten the cattle still more, and turn some of them back? But the men were still more alarmed at the sight of the stamping, lowing beasts and climbed up the steep banks out of the way until the slow progress was over.

Although difficult, Archie found the descent exciting. The one who hated it the most was Wally. He wasn't a good water-dog any more: where were the gentle, salty tides of Governors Bay, where he loved to splash and carry sticks? The stones made him footsore and he refused to move, howling dismally, so that Archie had to drag or carry him until his own arms ached.

It was nearly dark when they reached the first piece of ground level enough to make camp; which meant, in this steep country, just level enough to be sure of not sliding down into the river.

Three men, with horses, had already arrived there. They held back the first of the cattle and waited for the drover to appear;

and when they saw Archie, they wouldn't believe at first that *he* was the drover.

"You *must* have a mate!"

"Yes. My mother!"

This set everyone laughing and the men watched keenly for the appearance of this daring woman. But she was a long time in coming, and Archie and two of the men, Charlie and Isaac, went back up the gully to help her, leaving the third man to mind Wally and the mob. He had the unlikely name of Horace.

"Blimey!" cried Horace when at last Mrs Phipps appeared, dripping wet from her muddied lace collar to her heavy boots. "Is this the lady drover! Big things come in small parcels, I reckon. Well, lady, make the acquaintance of Horace!"

Mrs Phipps roared with laughter too.

"Oh, no! Not a Roman name – here!"

"Everyone laughs," sighed Horace. "I can't sober them up with five-pound notes."

The trio had been on the Otago goldfields and had missed their ship at Dunedin; so rather than wait for the next one, they had set out overland. They were originally from Australia and were delighted when Archie told them he was an Aussie too, and that Wally's name was really Wallaby.

"A good thing you didn't try bringing horses," said Charlie. "Mine got cast coming down that creek. Had to cut the girths to get him free. We might have to do 'em in and give 'em over for dog tucker."

The horses did look a sad sight. There was little enough food about to attract a bullock, and none to attract a horse; they had only a few sodden oats left in their bags.

The Australians had no tent, but had rigged up a shelter of

branches. In any case, the night was fine and there was a splendid camp fire where Mrs Phipps cooked damper for all five. Charlie helped Archie to pitch the tent, which meant cutting back some of the bushes to make room enough.

"I'll take my sleep first, Mother, shall I? And then I'll get out again for the midnight watch," said Archie.

The men stared.

"You chaps sailors – up here in the mountains?" said Isaac.

"We'll see 'em sailing off down river in the morning," teased Horace.

"It's to see the cattle don't go bush," explained Archie.

"You mean you stay up all night?" Isaac went on.

"One at a time. We've lost a cow already."

"Only one cow?"

"One too many," said Mrs Phipps.

"How if we took a turn?" said Horace. "Reckon I could teach a bullock his manners!"

"Can you count, though?" said Charlie.

"Enough of your chaff! If I see a cow going off, that's one cow, and if I see two, that's two!"

"You'll probably count every pair of legs, and double the herd for Mrs Phipps," roared Isaac. "Sit down, youngster; you can get a good night's sleep later on."

Archie needed no second invitation. The five of them crowded round the fire, only getting up from time to time to make sure that the horses and the cattle were where they were supposed to be. The poor animals were so weary that they made no move to roam, and Wally was quite enough guard for them.

"You drovers know a song?" asked Isaac.

So Mrs Phipps began in her strong, clear voice, while

Archie joined in with notes sometimes treble and sometimes bass and sometimes disappearing altogether.

"I'm a jolly little farmer, from Bedfordshire I came,
  To see my friends from Camberwell, and Morgan is my name.
  I've a dairy farm in Devon where I live when I'm at home,
  And if I get safe back again, from there I'll never roam.

"I lost myself entirely, I cannot tell you where,
  'Twas in a very lonely street, the corner of a square;
  A neatly-dressed young woman came walking up that way
  And long as I remember I'll ne'er forget the day."

The song went on through many verses to tell how he offered the lady his farm of forty acres, a horse and pig and cow; and they could spend their life on love and watercresses. He even gave her a sovereign towards buying her wedding dress, but alas, there came a letter telling him the sad truth.

"When next you ask a stranger into partnership for life,
  Be sure she is a maiden, not a widow or a wife!
  I've a husband of my own, and his name is Willie Gray,
  And if ever I can afford it, the sovereign I'll repay;
  But to think that I should marry you upon the first of May –
  You must have been as green as watercresses!"

"Bravo, bravo!" cried the Australians, and not to be out-done, in tones more enthusiastic than tuneful, they sang:

"It's in a first-rate business section
  Where four bush-roads cross and meet,
  It stands in a quiet and neat direction
  To rest the weary traveller's feet.

"Rows of bottles standing upright,
   Labelled with bright blue and gold,
   Beer so cold it needs no icing
   From the cellar's drear, dark hole."

Verse after verse followed to tell of the temptations – the
cards and bagatelle and the dancing girls and smiling darling
Nancy who "turns the tap, and thanks you for your shilling O".
But when the landlord of the "shanty" has fleeced the digger –

"Penniless you'll have to wander
   Many a long and weary day,
   Till you earn another cheque to squander
   In those shanties by the way."

They roared out every refrain, "the drear, dark hole", as if
they wanted to drown the roaring of the river; and occa-
sionally a morepork or a kiwi, or an unhappy cow, put in a
musical side-effect to the fireside party high up in the
mountains.

23

The Terrible Cow

AFTER a good night's sleep, Archie and Mrs Phipps rose to find that the Australians were as good as their word. The cattle had been well guarded; and the three horses were saddled and ready to leave.

"We'll watch out for that Bill of yours," said Horace cheerfully, "and pull him out of whatever mud-hole he's got stuck into!"

They rode off, leaving a bright fire for Mrs Phipps to cook her damper and bacon.

Going down the Teremakau was no easier, although the valley had widened and the river broadened as new tributaries swelled its flow. They were now in the true Westland forest. The awesome tales of the explorers were quite true. The

174

growth was so dense that Archie blunted his bowie-knife with cutting it back, and he had to use the axe. The supplejacks, which in Governors Bay made swings for Emma, were tangled into cattle-traps; and whenever a bullock got caught up, it was a hard job to cut him free as he bellowed and plunged. The river had to be crossed over and over again. The mob had to be driven in front, and Mrs Phipps would have none of Archie's idea that he should lead the first beast across the water, and encourage the others to follow.

"No, Archie! We take the pole and stick together. We'll take no chances with this 'terrible Cow'!"

"Then let me have the top of the pole, and break the current for you!" he said. And holding a second stick, he prodded the river-bed before him to make sure there were no holes to fall into.

This went on for three days. It was not possible to control every one of the cattle, and in any case some of them were weakening with the lack of their usual food. One bullock went missing, and another became caught in a snag at the river's edge and half-strangled, half-drowned himself. Archie cut him free and Wally, who was tired of eating wekas, had his first square meal in many miles.

Where the right bank of the Teremakau spread out towards Lake Brunner, there was a 1,200-acre stretch of pakihi. This area of rough grass, sedge and low bushes was known as the "Natural Paddock", and here the thirty-one beasts were soon ravenously biting at their first good feed on this side of the ranges. There was no need to watch them now.

The Paddock was a busy encampment, with several tents, a store, two grog-shanties, several horses, and numerous men –

but not another woman in sight. Diggers came hurrying round gallantly to pitch the tent for the lady. Many of them were "rough diamonds" who took special trouble to be polite.

Mrs Phipps decided to remain here for at least a couple of days while the cattle recovered their condition, and she and Archie rested and dried themselves out. At the same time she went round making inquiries. Would it be best to make a deal with some storekeeper, who would take the cattle on from here? Or where could she make a better sale? And had anyone, by chance, met up with a digger named Bill Phipps?

In reply to the last question, it seemed as if every second man on the goldfields was named Bill and not one of them answered to the description. As to the cattle, it would be most profitable to continue down the river. The sea-beach was the highway to Hokitika or the Grey where there were big and hungry townships.

But the last part of the route was the most dangerous of all; for the Teremakau was too deep and wide to be forded. They must either swim, or go in a boat with the risk of being over-turned in the rapids. If they preferred it, there was a land-route. It lay through a marsh like a mass of filthy black glue with rotting logs below and above its surface, and creepers as thick as enormous spider-webs. Mrs Phipps was sure that she did *not* prefer this way, for she would never get the cattle through.

"Mother, what did Mr Mahurangi say about this?"

"That only those who know the land are to be trusted. And that hasty tree-climbers often catch a fall."

"What does that mean?"

"It means we must be patient till we hear of a way."

Next morning Archie went down to study the river. Some

of the fords in the upper reaches were terrifying enough; but here the water sped by in great swirls. They must surely be "hasty tree-climbers" who would venture to swim it! Then he noticed something moving, far away against the opposite bank. It was a Maori dug-out canoe carrying several people.

Archie watched with growing excitement. Sometimes the canoe came towards him, sometimes it swung sharply the other way; first the current took it, then it shot across the current. In Lyttelton Harbour he had seen boats well handled in calm and in storm; his own brother Jack was as good at it as anyone – but he had never seen anything like this. The light craft was master in this violent river, and in the end it slid gracefully to its landing place only a few yards from where he was standing. Four diggers stepped ashore, leaving the canoe to its boatmen. Of course they were Maoris: a man and a woman.

"Tena koe!" cried Archie. "Your canoe is a bird of the sea!"

He was surprised to hear himself talking with a poetical phrase like Mr Mahurangi. The man answered with pleasure:

"Tena koe, e hoa! Ah! The gold has tempted a very young man today!"

"We've come with cattle, not for gold," said Archie. "You are Ngai-Tahu people?"

"You know Ngai-Tahu?" said the woman. She was young, not much more than a girl.

"We are neighbours at Rapaki. Mr Mahurangi told us –'

"Mahurangi!" she cried. "He my father's cousin! Did he speak to you of Ruia?"

Archie had to say no, but it made no difference to the warmth of their welcome; they stepped out of the canoe and shook his hands with delight. The man's name was Tamati.

When Archie told them about his mother they asked to see her at once.

From this lucky meeting came a sensible plan. Tamati and Ruia would take them down-river in the canoe, in careful stages. The cattle must sometimes be driven and sometimes be made to swim; so that part of the time, Mrs Phipps and Archie would be walking along the banks. Only the pack-bullock would be left behind.

The journey began that same day. Men gathered on the banks to see them off. "I'd liefer swim than go in that bit of bark," said a digger aloud, and others agreed with him and tried to persuade Mrs Phipps to come ashore.

"Stuff!" she said. "I think we've seen more of boats and boatmen than the rest of you. Do a good turn now, and drive the mob into the water for us!"

They were right to be confident. The Maoris knew every movement of the river. Just when a sheer cliff or a boulder loomed ahead, and Archie gasped aloud in spite of himself, the canoe would shoot neatly past or veer round into safe water. The only trouble was that they had so often to leave the canoe and push along the banks with the cattle. Still, the bullocks behaved well and only one stupid animal got himself stranded and lost somewhere among the gorges.

At last the river widened on to a shingle bed which stretched right down to the ocean beach.

There was another small settlement here, and a surprise. A dealer from Hokitika was waiting. Someone had told him that an extra fine mob was coming down. Could that "some-one" have been Charlie, or Isaac, or Horace? At all events he needed only to pass the word around and the butchers would send their buyers tomorrow to bid for the stock at auction.

The tent did not have to be pitched that night – indeed, it had been left standing at the Natural Paddock. There was honour among the diggers and although they might swear and drink and fight, they would never touch a tent. Archie and Mrs Phipps stayed in a Maori hut not far from the river and dined like royalty on baked fish and potatoes and fresh green cabbage; which somehow, after the travelling meals of rice and damper, tasted better than anything grown at Governors Bay.

Next day the bullocks and cows were sold for an average of £30 a head, which, after the auctioneer had taken his share, made more than £800 to be taken home across the ranges.

24

Home Again

FOR the return journey there was one worry, and one disappointment.

The disappointment was that no one knew anything at all about Bill Phipps. Always the same answer! Men spoke of Ballarat Bill, Japanee Bill, Bill the Shark, Brandy Bill, as if nobody had a real name any more; but no Bill Phipps.

"Maybe he's on to a lucky strike and he's not letting it be known where he is!" one of the diggers suggested.

So Tamati and Ruia took Mrs Phipps and Archie back to the Natural Paddock, where they must try to be away before the bad weather came again. They would move much faster without the cattle, and were feeling fit in spite of the strenuous walking and the wet conditions in which they had often slept.

But now came the worry. After Tamati and Ruia were paid – and Mrs Phipps insisted on that – and stores had been bought at the Paddock, there were still about eight hundred pounds in cash to be carried, with no possible way to conceal this from any lawless men upon the track.

"We must use our wits, Archie, for our knives won't see us far," said Mrs Phipps. Archie had to agree, although he had dreamt up some thrilling stories to tell the boys at Kaiapoi.

Once again, it paid to be patient. After two days, a pair of surveyors passed through on their way to Christchurch, and Mrs Phipps asked if they might travel together. At first the surveyors hesitated to take a woman, because she might not be able to keep up – but they changed their minds when they heard she had brought through a mob of thirty-four cattle, with only four losses. To prove that this was no hoax, the storekeeper took the surveyors and showed them the pack-bullock.

The men studied the heavy, stupid-looking beast without enthusiasm.

"I don't know how you kept thirty of those things on the move," said one of them, "for I can't figure out much progress with that one. Suppose you leave him here? We could put your tent on our pack-horse."

Mrs Phipps needed no persuading. She had no desire to push him through those boulders and mud-pools up near the Pass! The bullock was slaughtered and the best cuts of him made a feast for surveyors, storekeepers and diggers at the Paddock; while the tough parts made a feast for Wally.

The party of four made excellent progress.

At the Lakes Homestead, Mrs Phipps called to tell Mrs Taylor of their success, and to ask after the man they had rescued from the bush and sent on to her.

"He'll be safe in Christchurch by now, if he's managed to keep off the whisky," said Mrs Taylor. "Wait a moment!" She rummaged in a drawer. "He left a letter for the drover lady."

Mrs Phipps unfolded it and read its clumsy scrawl.

Dear Lady, was that Bill Fips you asked for cum from Guvners Bay and been at Gabreels Gully. Becos he was at Okarito last think I hurd & doing well he had good mates. But you stick to the cows they wont let you down like the yeller metal or the fiery likker.

Much ~~ob olig~~   Yours Mick Dorie.

With hands shaking from laughter and relief, Mrs Phipps passed the letter over.

"Poor man! He did his best to be polite, but he couldn't get round the 'obliged'," laughed Mrs Taylor.

"Excuse me!" said Mrs Phipps, and flung open the window on to the yard, where Archie was sitting on a gate. "Archie! Archie! Bill's at Okarito, and doing well!"

"Where's Okarito?" called Archie.

"Where is it? I haven't the least idea, but he's *there*!" cried Mrs Phipps, satisfied at last.

The Kaiapoi baker handed over his fresh, steaming bread and listened admiringly to Mrs Phipps. It was raining hard outside and it was just as well he could not hear the talk of the boys who crowded under the veranda to question Archie.

"How much money you get?"

"Nine hundred pounds, but there were cuts out of it."

"How much then? Ten – eight –" The boy was having trouble with his figures and Archie said, smiling:

"Eight hundred."

"Crumbs! Wouldn't they stick you up for that?"

Archie drew a deep breath and said: "They did."

"Who?"

"Two big dark foreign men. Might've been Spanish."

The audience was spellbound. "What did you do?"

"Went at them with my knife in one hand and the axe in the other."

"You never!"

"Show us your knife."

Archie unsheathed the bowie-knife and handed it over. The boys felt the blade and the point, which were now very blunt.

"It's got no edge any more," said one round-faced boy.

"Course not," said Archie scornfully. "It's worn down on the bones."

"What did your mother do?"

"Oh, she tied up their wounds so they wouldn't die, and told some diggers to tell the coppers."

Before the next question could come over, Mrs Phipps emerged with her bread.

"Ready, Archie?" she said brightly.

Her clothes looked the worse for wear, one of her boots was broken at the side, and her face was brown with wind-burn, but she looked as ordinary as anybody's mother and tinier than most of them. Archie whistled to Wally, nodded goodbye in an offhand sort of way, and walked off.

The boys stood in a knot and stared. It was hard to believe that this pair were such heroes. But they didn't meet heroes every day in the week, and they very much wanted to believe.

25

In the Orchard

A REAL-LIFE story can never have a real ending, because things go on happening to people, and people go on making them happen. On the other hand, a book must end somewhere.

It was a Sunday afternoon in February 1867, a little less than eight years after the Phipps family had landed in Lyttelton. Mrs Phipps was sitting outside the cottage in her rocking-chair: no packing-case seats for her now! Near by was Mary Ann, quite wrapped up in the book she was reading. From somewhere around came the voice of Emma, singing gaily, and adding her own musical accompaniment by whistling the verses all over again. She was working with her crochet-hook, for she had clever fingers: she had made the pretty lace front that her mother was wearing at this moment.

Today, for a wonder, there was no one else about. Visitors came often to see the garden, which had become famous, especially for its golden peaches: and these were ripening and scattering over the ground. There were plums too, red and purple and yellow; and greengages; and nectarines, and huge red apples. Rose and jasmine mingled their scents together, and a bellbird swung on the honeysuckle vines. Far above, the rocky peak of the Sugarloaf stood out in the strong sunlight to face the square head of Mount Herbert on the other side of the harbour.

Through a gap in the trees, Mrs Phipps saw Jack's cutter sail by. Archie and Jim and some of their friends were with him. It was a pleasure boat, but it was not considered right for picnic parties to hire it on the day for rest and worship. Jack was doing well as a boatman, Archie was making a good farmer and Jim could turn his hand to anything.

She picked a blue marguerite and turned it over in her hands. Whether she looked at the whole picture of her garden, the harbour and the hills, or only at this tiny perfect flower, it gave her a great contentment.

"Isn't nature wonderful!" she exclaimed to Mary Ann. "Everything in its season, everything for its purpose. I could sit here and read nature's book every day of my life!"

But Mary Ann, who was lost in a book with real pages, did not hear her. The voice that answered was Bill's.

"Happy, Mother?"

She looked round. "Yes, Bill! Very happy – but I thought you were away for the afternoon."

It was a while before he answered; and her keen eyes saw a familiar old restlessness about him. What was he after now? Not the goldfields this time! The West Coast had returned him with a few shillings in his pocket; but that was all. It was not his gold, but her cattle-dealing that had put the family on its feet.

"I want to ask you something," he said.

"Oh? What are you planning – a journey or a job?"

"Both, in one!"

"That means you're going to get married."

"Right on the nail, Mother!"

"Sarah Powell?"

"How did you know?"

"I can see as far into a stone wall as a good many masons." She added sternly: "You don't ask my permission."

"You wouldn't refuse it!"

"No, but I might warn Sarah," she teased. "You'll be taking her to the ends of the earth before you're through with life. I don't expect *you* to settle down quietly in Governors Bay."

"What if I don't? She'll stick by me!"

"No doubt she will. But, Bill," said Mrs Phipps, growing more serious, "there's one thing we must all think about."

Mary Ann looked up from her book, and Emma appeared with her crochet-work in her hand.

"I want to see if the collar will fit," said Emma.

"Trust girls to flutter round when there's talk of marrying!" said Bill. "You were listening."

"I couldn't help hearing," giggled Emma. "Poor Sarah!"

"What is the problem?" said Mary Ann.

"It's this. Is Sarah to be Mrs William Phipps – or Mrs William Small?"

Emma gaped. "Why should she be Mrs William *Small*?"

"Have you forgotten, Emma? Or have we kept the secret so well that you didn't even know? Our real name is Small. Now, is it right that Bill should be married under a name that isn't his own?"

"No," said Mary Ann promptly. "Sarah must be Mrs William Small."

"You used to be much afraid, Mary Ann, that we should be found out for running away!"

"Did we run away?" cried Emma. "Was that why we had to change our name?" But Mary Ann did not answer, and went on:

"There's hardly a chance now, Mother, and besides we're all grown up!"

"All?" laughed Bill as he took a pull at Emma's long plaited hair; but she ducked away and spun round on her toes with her dress flying, whistling a tune, and only stopped for a second to say, "Yes, I'm grown up! Look at me!"

"Thank goodness Sarah doesn't whistle," said Bill.

"Bill, I'm trying to be serious," said Mrs Phipps. "Mary Ann says Sarah must be Mrs Small. Well?"

"She can be Mrs Anything for all I care," said Bill cheerfully, "so long as she's *my* missus."

"And I say," said Emma, dancing herself to a stop, "that it will sound very silly if *he's* William Small and *I* am Emma Phipps."

"Well then," said her mother, smiling, "we'll stick together as we've always done. When Bill changes, we'll all change. We'll use our right name and we won't be runaways any longer."

And that is how the bells of St Cuthbert's first rang out for the Smalls of Governors Bay.

Historical Note

THIS story has kept to the truth about the Small family and their times, as far as I have been able to find it out, with guesswork and imagination to put life on to the framework of fact.

It was sparked off, for me, by two printed accounts: one by Clara Burrell in *Brave Days*, published in New Zealand's Centennial year by the Women's Division of Federated Farmers, and the other by Frances Cresswell in *Old Homes, Lyttelton Harbour*. This was drawn from the memories of Alfred Small who, like Mrs Burrell, was a child of Jim in this book.

Further researches have uncovered several inaccuracies in both these accounts, and where I have departed from them it is because I have made certain of the correct answer.

I have been favoured by the co-operation of many descendants of Mary Elizabeth Small and in particular by four of her grandchildren: Mr Alfred Small; Mr Charles Small and Mrs Emma Spence (both children of Archie); and Mrs Isa Greaves (a daughter of Jack Small) with her very rich and accurate memories.

The Governors Bay settlers mentioned were all real people, and so was Mr (later Sir) John Cracroft Wilson.

Of the many people who helped me with information, I must especially thank numerous descendants of the Small family; Mrs Frances Cresswell and Mr W. Wood, long associated with Governors Bay; Mrs O. C. Trembath from the Berrima district, New South Wales; Mr Arthur Munnings who lent me the Diary of Joseph Munnings; Mr R. C. Lamb of the Canterbury Public Library and Mr J. C. Wilson of the Canterbury Museum Library. I have found many useful books, also an unpublished M.A. thesis by Margaret Hunter called *Early Lyttelton from a Social Aspect*.

Finally I must thank those young readers who have given me all sorts of tips as the book was being written.

All this goes to show that it takes a great many helpers to make one book.